Kick a Stone Home

By the Author

A TASTE OF BLACKBERRIES

KICK A STONE HOME

Kick a Stone Home

Doris Buchanan Smith

Thomas Y. Crowell Company   New York

Designed by Andrea Clark. Manufactured in the United States of America

Library of Congress Cataloging in Publication Data. Smith, Doris Buchanan. Kick a stone home. SUMMARY: A shy fifteen-year-old girl, more at ease on the sports field than anywhere else, tries to cope with new feelings and a gradual understanding of herself, her divorced parents, and other people around her. I. Title. PZ7.S64474Ki [Fic] 74-4209
ISBN 0-690-00535-0

1 2 3 4 5 6 7 8 9 10

For
my mother
and
my daughter

Kick a Stone Home

1

SARA JANE walked home from school alone, kicking the same stone all the way. As her toe winged the stone from the top of the cinder bank at the back of her yard, Kay yelled.

"Hey, watch out!"

The stone whizzed past Kay's head. Sara made a face and turned it into a greeting.

"Oh, hi, Kay." Sara tried to sound cheerful. She half ran, half rode the rolling clinkers down the bank.

"What took you so long, Sara?" Kay asked.

Sara sighed and kicked at the grass. Now the stone would never find its place in the rock garden by the back door. It was dissatisfying not to complete the ritual.

"Oh, Miss Dickerson again," Sara answered.

"For goodness' sake. What now?"

Sara heaved her breath out again and Kay followed her to the house. Sara's brothers had preceded them; the door was unlocked. Sara traipsed in with her friend behind her.

"Did I tell you we have to outline the history book? The whole thing?"

"Yeah. But she's giving you several weeks to do it, isn't she?"

"Yeah, well." Sara plunked her books down on her bed and stripped her dress up over her head. Early spring in Atlanta was shorts weather, most days. Kay had already been home and changed.

Tally, Sara's Sheltie, came in with the leash in her mouth. Sara leaned over and took the leash and patted the little brown head.

"I have three chapters done, but I wasn't sure whether it was exactly what she wanted. I'm really terrible with outlines."

"I'll bet." Kay was teasingly sarcastic. When it came to schoolwork Sara usually did very well.

"No, really, I get all fouled up." Sara snapped the leash onto Tally's collar. "All that capital letter 'A,' small letter 'a' stuff." She put her door key into the pocket of her shorts in case Lowe or Donnie accidentally locked her out.

"After all the trouble I've had with her," Sara continued the explanation, "I thought it would be a good idea to show her what I had already done to see if it was okay." Miss Dickerson had been unfriendly to Sara since she had transferred out of her homeroom at the first of the year. Her transfer hadn't been anything personal against Miss Dickerson, it was just that Sara felt so shy. She hadn't known a single other student in that homeroom.

They walked across the yard and Sara saw Norman coming down the sidewalk.

"What did she say?" Kay asked.

"First, she said, 'I don't want three chapters, I want twenty-six chapters.'" Sara lapsed into an imitation of Miss Dickerson. At the same time she turned and walked backward, facing Kay and glaring at Norman over Kay's shoulder. The imitation of Miss Dickerson wasn't very good. But the effect of the glare on Norman was perfect. He crossed to the other side of the street, even though he lived on this side, two houses past Sara.

"You know, she barely looked at me." Sara walked frontward again, pacing her step to Kay's. Tally darted from side to side, giving everything the sniff test. "She just kept shuffling things around on her desk." Sara felt hot about Miss Dickerson but very cool about her power over Norman. Kay-the-observant hadn't even noticed.

"When I told her that I wanted her to check my outline, she said that my English teacher didn't teach history and she didn't teach English."

"You don't mean it!" Kay responded. They turned left off Tarleton Terrace, going a roundabout way to Kay's.

"When I think of the nerve it took me to even ask her," Sara added. She knew Kay's mind was on other things as soon as they turned the corner. There was a certain boy who had a certain paper route and Kay's eyes were already pretzeling down the curving street. Walking Tally was a convenient excuse.

"I don't see him. Do you see him?" Kay took Tally's leash from Sara.

Sara hadn't been looking. The whole thing was so dumb. She leaned over and picked off a long stemmed weed with a seedpod top. She looped the stem around itself halfway down the stem, collar fashion, squeezed it tight, and slid the collar quickly down the stem toward the head. The top of the weed popped off like a pebble from a slingshot.

"There's his bike," Sara said, nodding down the sidewalk.

3

"Where? Where? Oh, I see." Kay was all shivery excitement one minute and casual cool the next. She gave herself a just-happened-to-be-walking-by air.

The boy came out of an apartment building and hopped on the bike. He pushed off scooter fashion and rolled toward them. Kay nudged Sara.

"Well, another day another dollar," Kay said to the boy. Kay had maneuvered Tally between herself and Sara so that the three of them took up the whole sidewalk.

Sara mentally rolled her eyes. Flitter! If she couldn't think of anything better to say herself, she would keep her mouth shut, which is what she usually did anyway.

"Come on, now, Tally," Kay said. "Move over and let the boy pass." Kay barely tugged the leash and Tally gave instant response.

So did the boy. Right on cue he leaned over and patted Tally. He might as well have patted Kay for the pleasure she got out of it. Sara couldn't understand it for the life of her. It was a game. Surely this puppet knew that Kay was pulling his strings. Kay was exchanging words with Lochinvar. Sara looked at her shoes and pushed them against the grass that grew between the concrete hexagons.

Kay was so cutey-cute. It made Sara sick. If that was the way you had to act to have a boyfriend, then Sara didn't want one.

"See you around," Kay said, finally.

"Yeah, see you." He flipped down the kickstand and left the bicycle. He ran up and across several lawns tossing papers.

"He could at least progress a little and say he'll call," Kay mourned. "I'll give him one more week."

"It sounds like a sport," Sara laughed. "Three strikes and you're out. Four tries for first down and you lose the ball. Shape up or I'll send you to the showers."

"Oh, Sara. You turn everything into a ball game." Kay's

4

voice was sharp, venting her exasperation. Sara raised her eyebrows and said nothing.

"Oh, Sara, I'm sorry. I don't mean to hurt your feelings, but really, I do agree with your mother. I mean, it's okay to play football when you're ten years old, and even when you're fifteen if you play in a girlish way. But you. You play just like a boy."

"That's exactly what I intend," Sara said.

"Why do you have to act so tough, like nothing bothers you?"

"The coach wants me to cut my hair and come out for spring practice," Sara said flippantly, defensively, ignoring Kay's question. She didn't tell Kay how hard the boys were hitting in football these days. Someday she guessed she'd have to quit, but Kay's nagging, like her mother's, brought out her stubbornness.

Kay playfully punched Sara on the shoulder.

"You'll be okay. I don't know what I'm talking about." She handed Tally's leash back to Sara. "It's late and I have to go. See you in the morning."

Sara unhooked the leash from Tally's collar and commanded Tally to "heel." The little Sheltie trotted along beside Sara, looking up and wagging her tail. Sara bent down without breaking step and touched Tally on the head. She began to jog and Tally ran at her heels.

Sara rounded the corner to Tarleton Terrace. There was a moving van at the bottom of the hill. She kept her jogging pace.

"Hey, Sammy," Sara called as she approached the lot where the gang was playing football. "Who's moving in?"

"A boy."

"That all?"

"Well, his mother and father, dopey."

"Ugh. Another Norman?"

"Who knows?"

5

Sara wrinkled her nose. Norman was the spoiled brat of the neighborhood, the bully of little kids.

"So much for that." She stood first on one foot, then on the other.

"Well, I'll see you later," she said awkwardly, fumbling for a reason to walk on.

"You're not playing today?" Sammy asked.

"Yeah, Sara, come on," another boy said. "We've been waiting for you."

Sara grimaced inside herself but didn't let it show.

Her mother and Kay pulled her one way and the gang the other. How could she leave the gang? How could she retire from the game? They had been so nice about accepting her when she was new in the neighborhood. In that terrible year that she had, unknowingly, built so many walls between herself and others. Walls she still couldn't knock down. Baseball, football, basketball, only on the court or field had she felt at home.

"Let me take Tally home," she said. "I'll be right back." It was impossible to tell them. It was also impossible to play football with Tally around. Tally's herding instincts came to the fore when she saw a group of people running. She barked and nipped at heels until she was stepped on or tripped over.

Sara made a pretense of hurrying. Her timing couldn't have been less perfect. Miss Parmalee Dickerson was getting out of her car, which she had parked right in front of Sara's house.

"Sara Jane Chambers, you should be in that house working on your outline," Miss Dickerson said.

Outline, troutline, you old witch, Sara thought.

"Yes, Ma'am," she said politely, not slowing down. Miss Dickerson lived in the apartment building across the street. The moving van was taking up her parking space.

Sara crossed the screened porch, shoved open the door,

and let Tally go inside. She watched out of the corner of her eye while Miss Parmalee Dickerson with her bleached blonde hair and her too-fancy-for-school-teaching clothes disappeared into the courtyard across the street.

Sara had no sooner stepped back off the porch than a boy appeared from behind the moving van.

She had never thought about boys enough in terms of "opposite sex" to formalize an ideal. Yet there he was. He had light red hair and a slightly pug nose. At the sight of him a new kind of excitement charged through her.

Sara poised halfway down the stairs and watched him trot to the lot two doors away. Nervousness and unsureness overtook her. She went into the yard and swung up into her mimosa tree.

She had claimed the mimosa tree when they moved to Tarleton Terrace three years ago, just after her parents' divorce. It had been late spring and the tree was full of green feather leaves and pink powder-puff blossoms.

"Mom," she had said. "Can I have this tree?"

"Why, Sara Jane, it's in the yard. Of course you can have it. We can all have it."

"I mean really have it, for my own."

Her mother looked at her intently.

"Does it mean so much?"

"Oh, yes. I won't be selfish about it. Please?"

Her mother had put an arm around her shoulders and hugged her off-balance. Sara liked to remember the moment sometimes when she felt so far away.

"It's your tree."

It was more than a tree to Sara. It had become her nest.

At the second fork of the tree one branch stretched out almost parallel to the ground. Another reached upward just behind. It was perfect, the one branch for sitting on and the other for leaning against. When the branches filled out with leaves and blossoms, it was even a hideaway.

7

She was too old for a nest, fifteen. Just one more item on the list of things she was supposed to be too old for—like football and wanting to be a veterinarian.

Sara hunched down on her perch. The shouts and thuds of the boys having a raucous football game soared over from the vacant lot. When a play came out toward the street she could see Sammy commandeering the game. The new boy easily cradled one of Sammy's hard passes. A Norman he was not. Norman would have collided with the ball and run crying to his mommy.

The lot was by Norman's house, two doors up the long hill from Sara's. It wasn't a lot, exactly. Some long-ago city planner had planned a street that had never been cut through. It was the only place left to play since the woods had been replaced by more and more apartments.

Sara ached to watch the ball game at close range. She wanted to watch Him. But Sara was one of the star players. The boys would not let her get by with being a mere spectator. They would draft her into the game. Leaning her cheek on her hands, she tried to sort out her new feelings. She didn't know why, but she didn't want to be "one of the boys" with Him.

Of course, he'd most likely heard about her already. Sara Fullback, Sammy called her. But, if Sammy kept his mouth shut, the other boys probably would, too. Sammy was the lead tease, and off the field, the others didn't pay too much attention to her. If Sammy even guessed that Sara liked that boy . . . It made her shudder just to think about it. Sammy would never shut up that teasing mouth of his.

Her mother's voice from under the tree startled her. The time had slipped up on her. Usually she watched for her mother to turn the corner, coming from her job as manager of a real estate office. Then she would race inside and grab up all the odds and ends before her mother got down the hill.

"Sara Jane Chambers, I don't know what I'm going to do with you if you don't stop climbing trees and try to grow up." The same old line infuriated Sara.

"I'm not climbing. I'm just sitting." Nag, nag, nag. Sara heard her mother sigh. Their contentions with each other were continuous. She felt both guilt and pleasure that her mother did not know what to do with her.

"Well, come on in, now," her mother said.

Sara unwound herself from her perch. She helped with dinner and went to her room as soon as possible. She was awed by the suddenness of her new feelings. She needed to be alone.

She was most surprised by the fact that she didn't think of this new boy in terms of how fast he could run, how far he could throw, or how hard he could tackle. Until now, boys had been friends, buddies. Like Sammy.

She could hear Sammy now, teasing her. If only she could keep him from finding out. If only she could think of a good reason to quit football. Sammy and the boys wouldn't be likely to accept a feeble excuse and she couldn't tell them the truth.

She flexed her arm and felt the hardness of the muscle. Last week she would have matched that muscle with any boy on Tarleton Terrace, even Sammy. Today, she wasn't so sure she even wanted to try.

Sammy liked her, but he was the only one of the gang who ever talked to her about anything besides sports. Her mother said no boy would ever be interested in a girl who climbed trees and acted like a roughneck. Her brother Lowe wouldn't play ball if she was playing. Even Kay said she ought to change.

What did you do to get rid of a muscle? Would it

9

evaporate through disuse? She wondered. Or would she always have it? Was it to bulge there forever as a punishment for her refusal to be feminine?

Oh, flitter, muscles. If she was going to be a veterinarian, she would need muscles. Dr. Montini said it took a lot of strength.

Expelling a huge sigh, she went over and sat down at her desk. It was by the front window. With her chin in her hands she sat looking out at the light in the new boy's apartment.

2

IN THE morning she was late. She had sat up watching the light in his apartment until it went out. He had circused through her dreams. It was past eight o'clock. Kay would be gone.

Sara snatched up her books and hurried out. At the same time, he came tearing out of the courtyard across the street. A smile rose in her. He would have to cross to her side at the top of the hill.

All the way up the hill she kept glancing to see if he was noticing her. She wanted him to notice but not to notice that she was noticing. Her heart became a bass drum as she neared the top of the hill.

He crossed and wound up about three steps ahead of her. He gave no indication of knowing she was there. She felt like a dodo following him so closely, almost stepping on his heels. She would speak to him. She must speak to him. She pretended she was Kay.

"I see I'm not the only slowpoke this morning," she forced the words over the lump in her throat. Her voice was a little too loud. She felt her ears warm up beneath her ash-blonde hair.

"Hmm?" he said. He looked over his shoulder but did not slow his step. His profile was more perfect than she had imagined from her distant observation.

Sounding forceful to cover her uncertainty, she introduced herself.

"I'm Sara Jane Chambers. Welcome to Tarleton Terrace." She lashed herself inwardly for saying "Sara Jane." She was trying to become Sara, but the double name slipped out.

He slowed momentarily for her to catch up.

"I'm Giff, for Gifford, Proctor," he said. He cleared his throat after he spoke. A smile flickered crookedly. They walked in silence for a few steps.

Isn't he going to say anything else? Sara felt hot all over. She felt excited to be near him but stupid about walking along and not talking. The thrill was being stampeded by awkwardness.

"I know it's hard to learn everyone's name when you're new." She felt she was blurting her words. She was upset with him for not helping her. She'd made this much of a fool of herself, she might as well blunder on; perhaps she could plunge through the barrier.

"You've probably met my brothers, Lowe and Donnie. Donnie, anyway. A cute little brown haired guy with freckles?" She held out her hand to indicate Donnie's height.

"Yeah," he grunted. He walked determinedly onward, not looking at her. "I guess so."

"Look," he said, turning to look at her. She looked in

12

return and tried to swallow her nerves. "Look," he repeated. "I hate to dash off and leave you, but we're late and I'm going to run."

Sara was tempted to say "Huh?" but she had heard him very clearly. She gritted her teeth. Run, huh? In her mind she startled him by sprinting away. She anchored her feet into a rhythmic plod to keep them from following her vision.

"Yeah, sure. No need for both of us to be late."

Gifford broke into a jog and Sara visually paced him. She could have passed him with ease. There were no girls and only two boys she knew of who could outrun her.

Suddenly, before he was too far ahead for her to catch up, she tucked her books under her arm and began running. She tried not to think of his light red hair and his lopsided grin. He was a dunce. What did she care? He hadn't wasted much of his precious smile on her.

"Hi," she said as she caught up with him. "I can't afford to be late, either." She treasured his dumbfounded expression. Still running, she passed him and never looked back. She spent her classroom time thinking about him and between classes she searched for a glimpse of him.

After school she stalled at her locker instead of meeting Kay out front. Kay was too penetrating with her questions about moods and feelings. Sara wasn't in the mood to parry.

To avoid Kay in case she came looking for her, Sara walked slowly to the cafeteria and back. She tried to count her steps but her concentration kept breaking. Outside, a sun that promised spring to the world failed to lighten her mood. She held her cumbersome books in balance against her hip. She consciously sought out a smooth stone.

Take that, Miss Parmalee Dickerson, she said to herself. Take that, Gifford Proctor. If she added a kick for her father, she veiled the awareness of it.

13

She walked at a natural pace, sidling slightly to the left to be in position to kick the stone again. Soon the stone was a friend again, a companion on her solitary walk. There were certain rules she had developed about stone kicking. You walked along naturally and you never touched the stone with your hands. And, you tried to kick the same stone all the way home.

At the byway, she cupped the stone between the insteps of her shoes and hopped up the stairs. The byway, in a series of sidewalks and stairs, was a shortcut slicing through the center of the long blocks. It ended at the top of the cinder bank behind Sara's yard. When she kicked the stone through the air over the cinder bank, Kay yelled.

"Hey! What's with you kicking rocks? You almost took my head off with one yesterday."

Yesterday. That was a whole Gifford Proctor ago. There being no way, now, to avoid Kay, Sara skittered down the bank.

"Miss Dickerson again?"

"Mmmm." Sara let Kay deduce the wrong answer. Kay was trying to be a real friend. She was the only friend Sara had except Sammy since they moved to Tarleton Terrace. Since the divorce.

But Sara didn't share things easily. Even though she'd known Kay since last fall it was still a beginning friendship. Kay didn't even know that Sara's parents were divorced. Sara told Kay that her father traveled, which was true. But the implication that he was home on weekends was not true. Kay understood about traveling. Kay's father traveled, too.

Sara couldn't share Gifford Proctor, either. Not yet. Sara knew that Kay wanted to go walking. It would avail nothing, even if Giff came by, but she felt the need to keep a vigil.

"I don't feel like walking this afternoon," Sara said. "Let's just hang around out front."

"What's the matter?"

"I don't know. I'm just draggy."

"Well, everyone loves you when you're happy," Kay said cheerfully. "It takes a true friend to put up with a mope. What's-his-name will just have to do without me today. He deserves it!"

Sara pushed the back door open with her foot. She set aside the lid of the cake-saver with her free hand and speared a doughnut with her finger.

"Help yourself and put the lid back on," she said to Kay. Through the window she saw Dave Kellerman going down the driveway next door.

"Hello, Mr. Kellerman," Sara called, waving her doughnut.

"Who is that?" Kay asked with interest.

"Just a guy," Sara said. "A married ex-marine who is going to college. He lives in Sammy Carlisle's basement apartment."

"He surely is good looking." They both watched the young man until he was out of sight. Sara hunched her shoulders and gave a "maybe so" look to Kay's comment.

Dave Kellerman. That's who she could talk to about Gifford Proctor. Dave and his wife. Somehow Sara had been able to become friends with them and talk to them about real things. She didn't want to share the Kellermans with Kay, either.

Sara scrunched her face to squeeze away the guilt. Kay was really a good friend. But there wasn't much of her real self that she shared with Kay.

"What was that for?" Kay asked. Kay didn't miss anything.

"I was just thinking about when we first met." True

15

enough. Sara was thinking that even from the first she hadn't deserved a friend like Kay.

"When you chased me up the hill?" Kay asked.

"With a piece of rope." Sara smiled, thinking of her mischief.

"I was so mad at you."

They hadn't known each other then, last summer. Sara had been in her yard with a short strand of rope that Donnie had just mistaken for a snake. A girl was walking slowly down the street.

"I'll bet I can speed her up," Sara said, laughing to Donnie and Sammy. She made the rope writhe in her hands.

"A snake! A snake!" Sara shrieked, running toward the sidewalk. The girl turned to face Sara.

"Keep it away," she said. "Please keep it away from me."

Sara didn't stop. The girl ran up the hill, checking every few steps to see if Sara was still coming. Sara chased the girl until, screaming and crying, she didn't look back any more. She just kept running. Sammy was doubling over with laughter.

Later, Sara had been ashamed. She didn't know the girl. But she probably wouldn't have apologized anyway. When school started, the girl was in Sara's gym class.

"You're the girl who chased me with a snake," Kay had said.

"It was a rope," Sara replied. She was embarrassed and not able to utter an apology.

"That's what someone told me, later," Kay said. "I can't help it. I'm so afraid of snakes."

"I'm still afraid of snakes," Kay said now. "Or ropes that look like snakes!"

"I was amazed that you weren't still mad," Sara said. "I would have been furious."

"But that was weeks later," Kay said. "Over is over."

Sara wished she could let things be over. She let things simmer until the heat of them wilted her. She wanted to talk to Kay, to tell her about the divorce, about her strange new feeling about Giff, about stone kicking. The words played ring-around-the-rosy in her head, but they all fell down before they got to her mouth.

Sometimes she wondered why Kay even bothered with her. Kay was like Sammy. They didn't seem to mind that she was so stiff and slow to warm up and be friendly. Kay had been trying to be friends all year. But it was only lately that Sara had been able to open up and let the friendship develop.

Still, she couldn't talk to Kay about the important things. So she talked about school and Miss Parmalee Dickerson, and about dogs and the weather.

3

As she went up the hill to meet Kay, Sara locked her eyes in a straight-front position to keep from looking for Giff. She still felt humiliated from yesterday's episode. He'd have to make the next move and that would probably be never.

Kay stepped out with a yard-long camel stride. Sara had driven Kay like a drill sergeant until Kay had learned to swing her legs into a wider stride. Now, even though she would not allow herself to look, Sara was aware that Giff might be somewhere down the hill behind them. She didn't want Giff to see her galumping along. It was stupid, really, since she had outrun him yesterday. Just the same, Sara began limping.

"What's the matter?" Kay looked down at Sara's feet.

18

"I hurt my ankle last night," Sara lied smoothly.

"Well, I'm sorry, but hurry up and get over it. I've just spent months learning to walk faster."

The long stride was like kicking stones, automatic. Sara had used the hexagon pattern of the sidewalk to help lengthen her step, skipping every other section. Now she tried to figure a pattern for shortening it. Stepping in every section was like doing the Charlie Chaplin quick-step. She slipped a glance over her shoulder.

No Gifford. And tomorrow she'd be gone all day. They were going to her father's. She shouldn't have to go anywhere but home to see her father. She lapsed into brooding.

"Why are you so quiet this morning?" Kay asked. Sara remembered to keep up her limp.

"I was just thinking about my father." That was safe enough. Your parents didn't have to be divorced for you to be thinking about your father.

"Oh." Kay sounded rather abrupt.

Sara felt compelled to cover herself with words. She felt vulnerable, as though Kay could see through her.

"He's coming home tonight," Sara said. "He wants us to spend the day somewhere special tomorrow." The last part, at least, was true.

"Oh, that sounds great. Where will you go?"

"I don't know yet." Sara hunched her shoulders.

"At least he's home between trips." Kay sounded wistful. When she spoke again her voice was almost inaudible. "My father doesn't live with us."

Sara looked at Kay. If she wanted to find out something, Kay was shrewd. Somehow, Sara thought, Kay suspected about her father.

"What?" Sara asked, not venturing any information.

"Nothing," Kay said.

19

Usually Sara let subjects drop. But Kay was trying to sneak in, trying to find out something about Sara's father by telling lies about her own father. Sara pressed.

"Did you say that your father doesn't live with you?"

Kay tossed her black cap of hair and tilted her rounded nose into the air.

"Yes, that's what I said," Kay snapped. "You needn't be so snooty. My parents are divorced!"

Sara was so astonished that she couldn't say anything. They walked along in shocked silence. She glanced at Kay and saw something glistening in the corner of Kay's eye. Tension snapped within Sara and she began to laugh. Kay looked venomous.

"Mine are, too," Sara said, ripping the curtain from her holy of holies. "My mother and father are divorced, too." She said each word distinctly.

"There's certainly nothing funny about it," Kay retorted.

"I know," Sara said, laughing again. Her laughter was like her tears that day in the counselor's office when she had asked to be transferred from Miss Dickerson's homeroom. She couldn't seem to stop.

"I don't see what's so funny," Kay said again.

"It's just that," Sara gasped between chortles. "we have told each other so many lies about our fathers!"

Then, Kay, too, began to laugh—in spite of herself. They sat on a wall and put their books down so they could hold their stomachs. Tears squeezed out of their eyes.

Jean, a friend of Kay's Sara knew on sight, passed by.

"What's so funny?" she asked, looking puzzled.

Kay and Sara were unable to stop laughing long enough to answer. That started them full force again. Jean walked on, shaking her head.

"Can you imagine," Sara managed to spurt between

gasps, "what she would have said—if we had told her—if we had said we were laughing because our parents are divorced?"

Finally, they regained their composure. Still smiling, they hoisted their books just as Gifford came down the sidewalk. The spirit of the moment made Sara bold.

"You'd better run, You'll be late." Sara whooped again and Kay joined her.

Gifford looked at them wonderingly and laughed. He jogged a few steps. A car pulled up to the curb and some boys offered Giff a ride.

"Can I ride instead of run?" He smiled broadly as he stooped to get into the car. "Then I know you won't beat me." Sara didn't answer. Her laughter calmed into a smile. Her day was made.

"On the school records I put that my father still lives with us," Kay was saying. Kay-the-observant had not caught anything significant between Sara and Giff.

"I do, too," Sara responded.

"Why?"

"Why do you? You said it first."

They walked along quietly, now, through with their laughter and unable or unready to answer their own questions.

Finally Kay spoke.

"I guess because I still hope he will come home and I won't have to bother telling everyone and changing the records back."

"But, I don't understand why you never said anything about it," Sara said. "You always talk about—well, everything."

"I know, but . . . Well, I guess it was as though if I didn't talk about it, it wouldn't be true." Now that admissions had been made they stood boldly, like tangible objects, ready for inspection.

"How long have they been divorced?" Sara asked.

"Two years."

"Mine have been three years. Do you really think your father and mother will get back together?" It was a statement more than a question. Three years! She had not acknowledged or accepted the passing of time. It wasn't new and fresh any more. It was over. And, like Kay had said about the rope-snake, over is over.

Recognizing, at last, the finality of it released the latch on the pain and it roared through her again. Her mother and father would never get back together. He had been remarried for two years. It was wrong to keep on hoping.

"How did you act when they, I mean, when they told you?" Sara asked. "When he left?"

"Oh, they were separated so many times. Apart one week, together the next." Kay paused. "I wanted them to decide one way or another. But I had hoped they'd decide my way, to stay together."

"I pitched a tantrum like a little kid," Sara volunteered. "I screamed and yelled and wouldn't let him get out the door." Without realizing it, she had let a little of herself spill over onto another person.

She remembered with distress how she had tried to hold him. Her older brother, Lowe, had helped take her father's things to the car. She was supposed to help, but she wasn't going to help him leave.

She didn't believe he would really go. Somehow it was going to turn out to be some kind of game, a test, like the fire drills at school. He taught them not to panic and she was trying hard to keep calm.

Her baby brother, Donnie, was already asleep. She followed her father to the back hall when he went to say good-by to Donnie. Donnie was deep in a five-year-old's sleep and her father did not waken him. But the way her father stood there looking down at him told Sara the truth. She returned to the living room and confronted her mother.

"He is really leaving." Sara's voice was strained.

"Sara Jane, honey. I told you all about it."

"But he's really leaving!" Sara could not, would not comprehend. When her father came into the room he spoke quietly.

"Walk with me to the car, Sara Jane." He stood with his arm held out to her.

Sara could not move. Her father put his hand on the doorknob and turned it. She flew at him like a bat. She grabbed his arm and no amount of persuading would make her let him go. He pried her loose and she grabbed at his suit and tore the pocket. He pried her loose again and again until at last she was a sobbing heap on the floor, hanging desparately around his ankle.

"Didn't you prepare the child?" he said to her mother.

"Prepare? Prepare?" Sara screamed up at him. How could she have been prepared for such a thing? How did you prepare to have yourself torn in half?

"Do you want to go with your father?" her mother asked quietly from the corner where she was sitting.

"Go? I don't want anyone to go!" Sara wailed. "I want him to stay."

"What?" Kay asked, bringing Sara out of her memory.

"I wanted him to stay," Sara said softly. The laughter of release and sharing was gone. The relief had been transitory.

Sammy Carlisle chose that afternoon to try to pry. She had climbed into her nest, which was unshielded in the early bud of spring.

"For a girl who is growing up you are still a good tree climber," Sammy said, swinging himself apelike into the next best perch.

"Aren't you going to come play ball?"

23

"No," she said.

"You must have gotten your period," he said bluntly.

"Oh, I've had that, if it's any of your business."

"You have?" He seemed genuinely surprised. "I sure didn't know it. And I can usually tell. When a girl is having her period she misses a day or two of school or she goes to the clinic to lie down. And she goes to the rest room all day, checking."

"Well, it's no big thing with me. My biggest problem right now is Miss Parmalee Dickerson." She whispered when she came to the name, trying to draw Sammy off course. "It would be just my luck for Miss Dickerson to come by just now and hear me talking about her." It was surprising how often Sara saw Miss Dickerson now that she knew who Miss Dickerson was. Last fall Sara hadn't even known Miss Dickerson lived in the neighborhood.

"Yeah, I hear she's giving you a rough time," Sammy said. "Is that why you can't play football; you're too busy studying history?"

"That has nothing to do with it," Sara said, quickly regretting it. History and Miss Parmalee Dickerson was a ready-made excuse, one that Sammy was handing her.

"Then it's true. You are growing up." Sammy snickered. "Who's the boy?"

"Who says there is a boy, anyway?" Sara was piqued.

"Oh, Sara Jane, there's always a boy. Just like there's always a girl."

"What girl?" Sara asked with renewed interest.

"Oh, any girl," Sammy shrugged. "No particular girl. There are lots of girls."

"Like who?" Sara was determined to press, to not turn him loose until he answered, like he did to her.

"Well," he drawled and stalled. "Maybe not a *girl* exactly."

"A what, then?"

"A Miss Parmalee Dickerson," he said.

"Aaugh!" Sara gagged as Sammy burst out with his shotgun laughter. He reached out to jab her in the ribs.

"Who is it? Who is it? Who is it?" he taunted.

"Well, it isn't anyone you know, so you can just forget it!" She was irritated with Sammy and with herself. She swung down from the tree like a small monkey.

"Sara Jane's growing uh-hup," Sammy chanted behind her.

She stamped across the porch and slammed the door. She wasn't doing anything right. Why hadn't she told him about her ankle? She couldn't play football on a sprained ankle, and she had already established a limp. She should have acted casual with Sammy. He would watch her every eye-blink now, trying to find out who the boy was. And she had been foolish enough to admit there was one.

She secreted herself in her room and pushed the armchair in front of the door to block an unwanted entry. She stood in front of the mirror and looked at herself in disgust. The only good thing she could see was that she definitely was not flabby. She was hard and firm. Too hard, she thought. Too firm. She had worked at tree climbing and rough play to make her muscles show. And they certainly did. She pushed at her brawny arm. Her veins even showed.

She pulled her desk chair over in front of the mirror and practiced sitting. She had trained herself to sit with her legs apart, or with one foot on the opposite knee. It was torture to keep her legs together.

The home-ec teacher said that walking with a book on your head made you more graceful. Well, Sara could walk with ease with a book on her head, but she was about as graceful as a Great Dane puppy.

She stood with one heel at the instep of the other foot

and the feet almost at right angles. She felt like an absolute fool right here by herself. What would she feel like in front of people.

Sara knocked over the chair with vengeance. She picked up Tally's leash and shoved the chair from the door.

"Here, Tally. Come on, girl." Sara slapped her knees as she called. Maybe Tally couldn't understand, but neither did she make demands.

Sara abandoned her worn trail. She walked up the long hill of Tarleton Terrace and kept on walking until she felt she had holes in her feet through which her troubles could drain. She sat on a wall with faithful little Tally leaning against her.

4

IN THE MORNING when Sara heard the horn blow she jerked open several drawers and rummaged for her bathing suit. She chided herself for not having looked for it last night.

Donnie barreled through the living room and banged out the door. Sara found her suit and hailed Lowe.

"Dad's here." She got no response. Hunching her shoulders, she went out. There was Lowe, sitting in the back seat like little Lord Fauntleroy. Sara pressed her lips together. Lowe was first out, prompt and efficient. He hadn't bothered to call her.

"What took you so long, girlie?" Her dad leaned across the seat to kiss her as she got in beside Lowe. Lowe squeezed himself into the corner. Her thoughts were bitter, about Lowe her unbrotherly brother, but the words came out carefree.

"I had to find my bathing suit. You know me, last minute Lily." She didn't want her father to know she was angry with Lowe. Dad was upset when they didn't get along. She was afraid he'd say, "Okay, no swimming." That would leave them stuck at the apartment all day.

Donnie filled the gap.

"Are we really going swimming? Will you let me jump off the high dive? Where's Mama-Joyce?"

At the apartment Donnie bounded up the outside stairway and burst into the kitchen to hug Father's Wife. Sara felt the air stiffen when she and Lowe came in. Lowe didn't even speak. Sara at least said, "Hi," and stretched her lips across her teeth. She searched her mind for something to say.

"You look very pretty today," Father's Wife said.

"Thank you," Sara replied.

"Would you like to help me with these cookies?" F.W. asked.

Sara looked at Joyce's floured hands and the mounds of dough humped on the breadboard. She liked to pinch off uncooked cookie dough and mush it around in her mouth.

"Here, roll it out for me," Joyce said, extending the rolling pin. Sara could see through the timing of the cookie-bake. It was bait. F.W. was trying. Sara wanted to reach out for the rolling pin, but, instead, her hands found themselves behind her back.

"Maybe later," she muttered as she faded into the living room. She heard the thunk-thunk of the rolling pin and Donnie's happy chatter. Donnie the balm. Donnie the gullible. He would swallow anyone's bait. Sara thumbed through the magazines looking for something interesting to read.

"I wish we could talk." Her father's deep voice was edged with pleading. He came into the room and sat down.

"I thought we did," Sara Jane said.

"I mean about . . . things." He was fumbling and she couldn't help.

She was thinking plenty. Like, how did all this happen in the first place, and what are we doing here and what do I call your wife? Three years. She had vowed yesterday to let it be over, but she couldn't break the seal.

"Well, I'm still doing fine in school except for history. I have this dumb teacher, Miss Parmalee Dickerson. You should see the way she . . ."

"Sara Jane." He almost choked on her name.

Sara stopped rattling. She hated the look on his face. Agony. She widened her eyes as a guard against unwanted moisture and twisted her mouth cockily against loose blubbering. She was filled with hot liquid pain.

Her father's expression remained unchanged. Sara felt a pounding in her chest as if a miniature wrecking machine was rumbling around inside her.

She felt a tear on her cheek. Swiping at it with one finger, she slammed the magazine down and moved to the window. Lowe had the right idea. He was miserable, too, but he was outside, miserable alone. He was tossing up that infernal baseball and catching it with the glove that hung like a growth on the end of his left arm.

"Are we going swimming, Dad?" Sara kept her back to him. Swimming, baptism, salvation. If her eyes were red she could blame it on the chlorine.

She heard him sigh. He must have a wrecking machine inside, too. She had been so absorbed in her own hurt that she had not wanted to see his. Just turn around, she told herself, and tell him you understand. Tell him you don't mean to make things hard for him.

29

"Yes," he said finally. "We'll eat lunch down at the 'Y' and swim. Then we'll come back here for supper. I'll get Donnie."

Tell him now, before he goes. She visualized him getting up with his hands braced against his knees, the way he did. Her lip was raw from chewing it, but she couldn't release the catch in her throat. In a minute, he left the room. She raised the window and called, pseudo-gaily, to Lowe.

"Hello, Lowe, there below. Do you have your suit, you brute?"

Lowe glanced up with his most withering look and didn't answer. That was par for Lowe. He was under the certain conviction that he would be struck with a plague if he acknowledged her.

As she picked up her bathing suit from a chair, she saw Lowe's suit and took it also. Imbued with a weird sense of victory, over F.W., over her father, over Lowe, she loped into the kitchen.

"We'll see you this evening," she said casually to Father's Wife. "If we don't drown."

"Don't do that," F.W. said softly. "I'm planning a big dinner and I'll need you to eat your share."

Sad, sad. F.W. is as glad to have us go as we are to leave. How did things get so tangled? Feeling a rush of sympathy for F.W., Sara banged out the kitchen door and clattered down the stairs.

With her finger and thumb she lifted Lowe's bathing suit and held it away from her.

"I hope I haven't contaminated myself," she said to Lowe. She wasn't about to save him a trip upstairs without adding a gibe. He snatched the suit from her without a word. Dad and Donnie had come down the inside stairs. They all piled into the car.

To keep from meeting any eye, she gazed at the apartment building. An old stone house, almost a mansion, it had been remodeled into apartments. It was the kind of place that Sara would like to own the whole of and ramble around in by herself.

"Do you really own that mausoleum?" she asked her father, putting as much derision in her voice as possible.

"Yes," he said. "Sometimes I wonder about it myself." He laughed.

"Well, I like it," Donnie said. "I like the high stairways and the stones that make it look like a castle."

Lowe, of course, didn't say anything. Donnie kept up his childish patter. He wanted to hear why, if it was the Young Men's Christian Association, Sara was allowed to go.

"She's young, isn't she? And a Christian?" Dad winked at Sara.

They pulled into the parking area behind the "Y." It was one of the newer ones built on the family concept. For Young Men or not, it was no longer for men only, or, even, the young.

Walking briskly across the parking lot, she hurried to change. She was anxious to feel the water around her.

Upon entering the pool, she swam its length. As she emerged at the other end something hit her with a splat.

"Rag-tag, rag-tag," said a laughing Donnie as she peeled the wet T-shirt from her head and shoulders.

"All right, you little monster. Get in the pool so I can get you." Out of the pool was "base," and Donnie was the only one allowed base.

"Get Daddy, get Daddy," he shouted, pointing. She looked just in time to see her father disappearing under the water.

"There he goes, there he goes," Donnie called. From his vantage point above the pool he was able to follow Dad's progress.

"Will you shut up saying everything twice," Sara shouted. With the shirt flapping in her hand, she struck out, swimming in the direction Donnie indicated. When Dad surfaced, she was close enough to smack him with the shirt.

She was grateful for their rule against re-tagging the one who had just tagged you. He would have had her easily. Instead, he searched the pool for Lowe, who watched warily from the deep end.

In the shallow end Donnie now splashed and yelled, "Get me, get me!" He was still creating his own echo.

Just before Donnie reached the point of frustration, Dad called the game to a halt.

"I challenge you to a diving match," Lowe said to Sara.

"Who'll judge?" Sara asked. They both looked at Dad.

"I'll be glad for a chance to catch my breath," he said. They pulled themselves out of the pool and walked to the deep end. Dad sat on the side of the pool, dangling his feet in the water. Donnie sat beside him doing the same.

"Try a jackknife," Dad said.

"I can't do that," Sara said.

"Sure you can. Touch your toes. Let me see you touch your toes." Obediently, Sara leaned down and touched her toes.

"See, that's all there is to it, except instead of standing back up, you keep your head down and kick your feet up."

Lowe was on the board, ready. He took one step, sprang, and went up and out. Bending at the waist, he touched his toes. One leg flopped as he entered the water.

"There, you see?" Dad said, encouragingly.

"He already knew how to do it," Sara said.

"No, I didn't," Lowe said, shaking hair from his face as he came up.

Sara moved to the end of the board and planned her

moves. In her mind, she followed Lowe. But she wasn't going to let her leg flop.

Off she went. Lowe seemed to have had time for everything, but she was rushing toward the water. With her hands, she managed to tap her knees before she spraddled every-which-way into the water.

"That was a start," Dad said when she surfaced. Sara laughed. She must have looked like an Afghan hound puppy, legs akimbo.

"You have to spring," he said. She was thinking the same thing. Sammy could jackknife from the side of a pool. The few times Sara had tried it had been just as disastrous as this most recent attempt.

Lowe entered the water beautifully this time, almost at right angles, his legs straight and together.

"Come on," he said. "You can do it." The spirit of amity was so unusual that she wanted to do it, for him.

Again she left the board. This time she touched her shins and landed a little less askew. In a few more tries, with Dad and Lowe cheering her on, she found her toes and entered the water at least at a smooth angle.

Donnie, bidding for his share in the fellowship, interspersed the dives of his older brother and sister with cannonballs.

Tired of diving now, Sara cut through the water, alternating the crawl, sidestroke, and breaststroke.

When her father called, saying it was time to go, it was like being startled out of a pleasant dream and trying to nestle back into sleep to catch the fragments.

"Just a minute," she called, skimming across the water and plunging into a surface dive. Gliding under the water, finning like a fish, kept reality away.

A lump settled in her throat as though she was already eating dinner with F.W. Could she tell him she didn't feel well? Could she pretend cramps? Coming up, she hoisted

33

herself onto the side of the pool and sat there enjoying the feel of the water streaming down her body.

"Hurry up, Sara," Dad called. "Why do you always have to be last?"

Short memory, she thought. He carefully recorded all of her lasts and conveniently forgot her firsts. They were all waiting at the car by the time she dressed. The knot remained in her throat.

The pool had been comfortable territory, familiar ground. But now it was back to the mausoleum where she didn't know where to put her feet or her words.

"Just in time," F.W. greeted them. "Sara, darling, will you put the glasses of tea on the table, please?"

All the lithe grace of swimming vanished. She splashed tea on the table with the very first glass.

"That's quite all right," Joyce said, coming right behind her with a dishcloth. As they ate, Dad and Joyce and Donnie chattered casually. Lowe spoke only when asked specific questions about baseball.

"We have my cookies for dessert," Donnie bragged. "You could have helped, too," he said to Sara.

"Maybe she will next time," Joyce commented, smiling. Yes, that was the worst part, Sara thought. There would be a next time.

5

RIGHT after supper, mercifully for Sara, Dad took them home. She could hardly wait to get her hands into the comfort of Tally's fur. She'd get the leash and she and Tally would go for a long restorative walk.

After kissing Dad good-by, she was on the porch before he drove away. Mother was waiting just inside the door. Sara often wondered if her mother peeped out for glimpses of Dad as she herself looked for Gifford Proctor.

"I heard the car," Mother said. Sara was embarrassed. There was no need for her mother to explain. "I've been waiting for you, Sara."

Her mother put a hand behind Sara's head and pulled her close. "Sara Jane, sweetheart," she said. "Tally is hurt. She was run over."

Startled, Sara jerked away, uncomprehending.

"She slipped out when I went to get the mail. I called her back but she wouldn't come. She must have been looking for you."

Sara's chin quivered and her eyes glossed over. Tally hurt?

"But she always comes when she's called," Sara said.

"She didn't come this time, Sara Jane," her mother said softly. "She ran right in front of a delivery truck. Sammy helped me take her to the vet. Dave Kellerman drove us."

"How badly is she hurt?"

Mrs. Chambers hesitated.

"Will she be all right?"

"We don't know, Sara. Dr. Montini said he'd do his best."

"Can I go see her?" Sara asked.

"Not tonight, Sara Jane. Dr. Montini said to call tomorrow at one."

"One? That's half the day," Sara cried.

Sammy knocked at the door and came in without waiting.

"I'm so sorry, Sara Jane," he said. His arms moved out in a gesture of helplessness. Sara sniffed and touched the corner of each eye with her finger tips. She walked past Sammy, out the front door, and he followed.

"Will she be all right?" Sara asked, stopping at the steps. Sammy knew a lot about animals and she expected a magical, healing answer.

Sammy shrugged.

"How can I wait until one o'clock tomorrow to find out?"

Sammy shrugged again.

"I'm going to call him right now." She turned.

Sammy put a hand on her arm, restraining her.

36

"Look, why interrupt him with telephone calls?"

"Wouldn't you, if it was your dog?" She sat on the top step and leaned her face onto her knees, crying.

"Oh, Sara, I'm so sorry." Sammy stretched his arm across her back. She felt its warmth and it emphasized the need she felt, the need for someone's caring. For a moment she cried harder, then she muffled it.

"I'm sorry," she said. "It's not just Tally. It's everything."

"Everything?" Sammy questioned. "What else?"

"Oh, my mother and father. You know."

Sammy looked surprised.

"That's been a long time," he said. "You mean it still bothers you so much?"

"I have to live with it, you know. Every day."

"Do you think about it every day?"

"No. Not every day, but every week, at least, when we go to see him."

Sammy shook his head, not understanding.

"Would it be easier if you didn't see him?"

"No!" Sara said emphatically. She stared at Sammy. How could he even say such a thing.

"I could think of things, too, Sara Jane. At least you get to see your father once a week."

"But you were just a baby. You didn't even know your father." Sammy's father had died before Sammy was a year old.

"I know him. We have pictures. My mother has told me all about him. I love him, too, you know. Don't you think I have missed not having a father?"

"You mean you'd rather have your father alive and divorced from your mother?"

"Alive, anyway," Sammy said. "Would you rather have yours dead?"

37

Sara lay in bed with her hands behind her head. Of course she didn't want her father dead. She had to admit that she had thought on occasion that it would be easier to grieve for a dead father than a divorced one. But, no. She wouldn't prefer him dead.

But she didn't like seeing him only on weekends, either. She needed a father every day. And now, with Tally hurt, she felt even more alone. There was no comfort anywhere.

Where was God? Why didn't He help her? The only relief it seemed would be to crawl into her tree. But that would really rack it up, climbing trees late at night. That would be just what she needed, to be called loony on top of everything else.

She slept fitfully. Thinking of Tally, hurt and alone and not understanding, only increased her own misery. Now that it was positively too late, she wished she had called Dr. Montini. How could she wait until one o'clock?

At eight-thirty, just after her mother had waked her for Sunday school, she called Dr. Montini.

"He's not in just now," a voice said. "Can I help you?"

Sara wilted. How could the doctor leave Tally? Shouldn't he be with her every minute?

"Well, I," she began, trying to talk without crying. "This is Sara Jane Chambers, the owner of the little sable Sheltie who was run over yesterday."

"Oh, yes," the voice said, then stopped.

"Well, I was wondering how she is," Sara said.

"Why don't you call the doctor at one o'clock for a report." Pain lurched through her at the dodging of her inquiry. She gripped the phone tightly, aware that her mother was watching her from the doorway.

"Is she . . . is she still alive?"

"Oh, yes," came the voice quickly. "I just looked in on her and she's doing as well as can be expected."

Suddenly Sara realized that she had not asked her

mother or Sammy what Tally's injuries were. She scraped her lip between her teeth and decided to wait for Dr. Montini to tell her.

"Okay. Thank you very much." As though the telephone itself were capable of being hurt, she placed the receiver gently into the cradle.

"Do I have to go?" she asked, turning to her mother. She meant to Sunday school, which she hated. She talked to God a lot, but church was just too much. Sometimes she wondered if God was ever there, at church.

"Yes, I think you should, especially this morning." Sara thought her mother treated church as a habit. I'll pray for Tally, she started to say. But she was thinking it sarcastically and her mother didn't like sarcasm about religion. Sara didn't think God was going to do anything about Tally. If He was, He should have kept her out of the street yesterday.

She mulled over the idea of being sick. Cramps again. She could fake her mother out any old time, but then she would have to play it out all day. Her mother would catch on if she had a miraculous recovery at twelve o'clock.

Getting dressed, she slipped into her pantyhose. That was better than wearing a stupid garter belt and having those metal tabs press circles into your legs. She stuck her feet into her comfortable loafers until time to go. She had been pressured into dressing up more on Sundays. All the other girls had been doing it since they were eleven or twelve. Flitter. God didn't care about your raiment, it was people who cared about that.

She was still messing around in her room when her mother called that it was time to go. She kicked off a loafer and stuck her foot into a flat-heeled brown pump. She grabbed her Bible. See the lovely family, Sara thought with sarcasm. See the lovely family go to Sunday school. She forgot the second shoe.

Mother and Donnie walked along together. Lowe walked ahead and Sara walked behind. There wasn't room on the sidewalk for them all to walk abreast. Lowe would not be caught walking with Sara, anyway.

Crossing a street, Sara scampered around Donnie and Mother and fell into step beside Lowe. Lowe gave her a look of disgust and stood aside for Donnie and Mother to pass, leaving Sara in front by herself. Sara twisted her mouth to keep the smugness from settling. She loved annoying Lowe.

Their footsteps were scrambled sounds on the sidewalk. We don't even walk together when we walk together, Sara reflected. Mother pays attention to Mother. Lowe pays attention to Lowe—and baseball. And he didn't appreciate Sara's virtue on that score. He tossed the ball high in the air to himself or disappeared to some hinterland far away from Tarleton Terrace and Sara.

Donnie. Well, Donnie was a charming pest. He was the glue. He was what held them all together.

In class, Sara sat quietly while discussions about school, parties, and clothes circulated the room. These were normal fifteen-year-olds. Sara was ten or forty-two, she couldn't decide which. She felt like a stranger.

"Oh, look," someone said. "Look at Sara Jane. She's being initiated."

Sara looked up in surprise. She looked to see if there was a visitor named Sara Jane. Everyone was looking at her feet.

"What club?" someone asked.

Sara looked at her feet. She had on one flat-heeled brown pump and one scroungy brown loafer. She kept looking at her shoes to keep from having to look up.

"What club?" they asked again amid the buzz and chatter.

"No club," she said. She felt the heat in her face and knew it was redder than a winter sunset.

"No club? Then, what?"

"I just goofed. I had my loafers on and never finished changing, I guess." She tried to laugh but her voice cracked.

"Aww. She's in a club. Initiation is supposed to be a secret. She'll get penalized if she tells."

The gabble around her continued while the temperature of her face increased. Her heart was pounding at the base of her throat in between her collarbones. She didn't know what would be more of a spectacle, sitting there or fleeing.

As the teacher began the lesson, Sara could not sit any longer. The little snobs, probably wondering what sorry club would have Sara Jane Chambers so they could be sure not to join it.

She jumped up from her chair and left the room without a word.

"Sara Jane," someone called, but she didn't stop. She ran down the halls and stairways of the church and out onto the sidewalk. When she hit the cool air she realized she had left her sweater on the back of the chair. She didn't go back.

She ran to the corner and hurried across the street and up the stairs into the byway. She sprinted down the sidewalk, down the stairs, across the street, and up the stairs until the byway funneled her down the hill into her own backyard.

The back door was locked. She pulled her key out of her pocketbook and ran around to the front. Giff was on the sidewalk in front of her house.

"Hello, Sara Jane," he said.

"Oh, shut up," she spewed. She turned her back on him,

fumbled with the key, slammed the door behind her, ran to her room, and fell across the bed, crying.

When her mother came home she had Sara's sweater.

"What in the world, Sara Jane," her mother said after knocking at her bedroom door. At least her mother knocked and didn't come plunging in like Donnie. Sara took a deep breath.

"Didn't they tell you?"

"They just said you went tearing out in the middle of the lesson and left your sweater."

"Well, see how they have exaggerated it already? The lesson was just starting, so it couldn't have been the middle of the lesson."

"Well, why, anyway?"

Sara had been reading. She let the book fall out of her hands and swung her legs over the edge of the bed. Four shoes were flopped by her bed. She stuck one foot into a dressy shoe and the other into a loafer. She held out her feet.

"What are you getting at, Sara Jane?"

Sara wanted her mother to be kind and concerned but, somehow, when she got what she wanted it was not what she wanted.

"I'm getting at that I went to Sunday school like this," Sara snapped.

"Well," her mother smiled. "Is that so terrible?" For once, the tone of her voice and the shape of her smile were exactly right. Sara smiled, too.

"I know. But it seemed terrible this morning. I was so darned embarrassed I wanted to cry, so I just left." She said nothing about the club business. The storm was over. She couldn't imagine why she had cared even for those few minutes.

Her mother sat beside her on the bed.

"I guess it was overreaction from being upset about Tally," Mrs. Chambers said gently.

The perfect moment was over. Of course she was upset about Tally, but Tally had nothing to do with a bunch of prissy girls laughing at her.

"Yeah," Sara said. "I guess so."

"Have you called about Tally?" Mrs. Chambers asked.

"It's just twelve-thirty," Sara said. "Besides, I'm thinking about going over instead of calling." Hearing about Tally over the phone would not help her heart. She wanted to see the tan face and feel the thick fur.

"Well," her mother said slowly, but before she got to what was going to follow, Sara was up and gone.

6

Sara banged out the front door and ran over to Sammy's.

"How're you getting there?" Sammy asked after she had asked him to go with her to Dr. Montini's.

"Ride bikes," she said. "Or walk." It was five or six miles to the vet's and no bus ran that way on Sunday. But she'd walked farther than that plenty of times.

"What I really had in mind," Sara said, leaning over the bannister and looking down the driveway toward the Kellermans' apartment, "was seeing if we could get a ride."

Sammy opened his mouth and nodded his head.

"Come on," Sara said. "I need to thank Mr. Kellerman for taking Tally to the vet." Both of them climbed over the railing and jumped into the driveway.

The Kellermans welcomed them heartily, as always.

Mrs. Kellerman had iced tea ready for them before they could refuse.

"Please don't thank me," Dave said. "How is she doing?"

"I don't know yet," Sara said. "I'm going out there in a few minutes. Sammy and I."

"How are you going?" Kellerman asked. He knew the Chambers did not have a car.

"Bicycle, I guess," she said. "It's not too far."

"Well, now," Dave Kellerman stood up, looking at his wife. "Why don't I run out to the drugstore now for that prescription? I can drop them by the vet's, then pick them up on the way back."

Sammy nudged her and she put her foot slowly but firmly down on his.

"That would be great, Mr. Kellerman," Sara said. "But we don't want to put you to any trouble." She felt like a fraud and she hated feeling that way with Mr. Kellerman.

"Yeah, Dave. That sure would be nice," Sammy said. "Sure would save a lot of pedaling." He wiggled his foot out from under Sara's.

"And what do I have to do to get you to call me Dave?" Dave asked Sara.

Sara ignored the question. In her mind she called him Dave. But he was an adult and married. She felt more comfortable calling him Mr. Kellerman.

Waving good-by to Mrs. K., Sara followed Sammy and Dave out to the old Mercury. She piled into the front behind Sammy.

"She's not ready for me to tell it," Dave said as he backed out of the driveway, "because she's having a little trouble. But we're going to be having us a little ole baby."

"Really?" Sammy and Sara said it at the same time. Dave's face was shining with happiness.

At the vet's, Dave planned to meet them in thirty minutes. Sara was sure thirty minutes wouldn't be long enough to spend with Tally. Maybe Sammy could go on back and she could get home later.

Dr. Montini startled her by opening the door just as she lifted her hand to ring the bell.

"Hey, come on in," he said, just as if he was expecting her. "Hello, Sammy."

The doctor led them through the short, narrow hall, past the reception room and office, through the examining room to the kennel area. Sara liked the sparkling look and the antiseptic smell of the place.

"Your little Tally is in pretty bad shape, I'm afraid," he said. He opened the last door and put his arm around her shoulder. Instead of the warmth she had felt from Sammy last night, she felt a chill.

"She may not make it," he said. Sara's eyes scanned the cages quickly. Everything that wasn't a sable Sheltie was passed over.

When she spotted Tally, her fingers slipped through the wire before Dr. Montini could unfasten the cage door. The dog lifted her head and strained toward the fingers.

"Remember, she will gauge your feelings," the doctor said. He opened the door and put his hand on Tally's head even as Sara touched the small face.

"Oh, Tally," Sara crooned, choking back the sobs as stinging tears splashed from her eyes.

"Hey, there, Tally girl," Sammy said. His voice sounded calm and soothing. Sara swallowed. Tally's tail thumped feebly. Sammy and Dr. Montini stood back and made room as Sara put her head into the cage and leaned it against Tally's head. Tally gave a high whine, of relief, or of pain, or of wondering why it had taken Sara so long to come.

"I'm afraid the internal injuries are massive," Dr. Mon-

46

tini said quietly. Sara raised her head and it bumped the top of the cage. Tally licked her hand.

"What do you mean?" Sara asked.

"Sara, Sara, you shouldn't have come," Sammy said, shaking his head sadly. "You should have called."

"I'm all right, Sammy."

Dr. Montini took both of her hands and put them together in one of his. "Sara, it would be a kindness to . . ."

Sara closed her eyes.

". . . put her to sleep. If she wasn't yours, I would have done it already."

"Why mine?" Why would he treat her animal any differently?

"I knew you would want to see her. And she, you."

The lump she'd been having trouble with ever since leaving the swimming pool yesterday threatened to choke her. She put her hand back into the cage and rubbed Tally's brow, muzzle, and ears. Oh, Tally, she thought. Why didn't you come when Mom called?

"Will you do it now, while I'm here?" Sara asked.

"I'll do it as soon as you leave," he said.

"No. I mean, I'd like to be with her so she won't feel alone." Her mouth moved in uncontrolled twisting.

"Are you sure?"

"Sara Jane?" Sammy questioned.

With a big sniff, she cleared her nose and gained control of her mouth.

"Yes, I'm sure."

Dr. Montini disappeared for a moment and Sammy acted frozen. Sara rubbed Tally and talked softly while Dr. Montini gave her a shot. Sheltie-like, Tally pushed against Sara's hand. Then, in a moment, she relaxed and breathed deeply.

"That's all," Dr. Montini said, easing Sara away. "She

won't know anything else. I'll take care of everything for you."

Sara stood quietly fanning her eyes with her hands. She thought of asking to take Tally home, to bury her, and decided against it. What was the use of a grave? She would have Tally in her heart always. She didn't ask Dr. Montini how he would "take care" of everything. Instead, she began asking about the other dogs.

"What's he here for? What happened to this one? Will she be all right?"

Dr. Montini introduced her to the other dogs and related their cases. In spite of herself she grew interested.

"You'll make a good veterinarian, Sara Chambers," the doctor said.

She flushed with the compliment. A question surged in her—could I work for you?—but she squelched it. He knew of her interest. He was probably just being nice because of Tally, she thought. If he needed someone, and wanted her, he would ask her, wouldn't he?

A buzzer sounded and Sara and Sammy jumped. Dr. Montini stepped through the door, leaving it swinging behind him.

"Dave, I bet," Sammy said, catching the door on the swing and holding it for Sara. She moved through it, pretending she was Montini's assistant. She trailed him through the examination room, past the reception room and office and down the dark hallway. Dave Kellerman was at the door.

At home, Sammy talked her into going to the movies. "I don't have any money," she said.

"That's okay. My treat," he said. Mother even waived her "no movies on Sunday" rule and said okay.

"I surely was surprised at the way you acted toward

Giff this morning," Sammy said as they walked up the hill.

"Giff?" She blushed when she remembered storming home from Sunday school. She had told Giff to shut up. She bit her lip and giggled.

"Who told you about that?"

"I was with him and you didn't even see me." Sammy talked on, trying to keep her mind off of Tally. "I had decided that Gifford Proctor was the boy. You quit playing football just when he moved in."

"That was just a coincidence." She was surprised at how easily she lied to him.

"Well, I think he likes you," Sammy told her.

"I certainly don't know why!" She thought of herself outrunning him, then snubbing him. But her pulse quickened and she waited for Sammy to say more.

"Sara Jane Chambers, don't put yourself down," Sammy scolded her. "When you stop putting on acts and are just yourself, you're a darned nice person." Sara involuntarily blinked her eyes as she cocked her head and smiled at Sammy.

"That's the way," he said. "That's the way to look at people, like you're alive and interested." Sara held the look and tried to record the position of each facial muscle.

She walked around looking at the photographs outside the theater while Sammy bought the tickets. Inside, he bought her a pack of Necco Wafers. When they were seated she excused herself. She hadn't been to the bathroom since before she left home for Sunday school and she didn't want to have to go in the middle of the picture.

The smell of perfume and hair spray assaulted her nostrils when she pushed open the door to the rest room. Just like school. There were girls lined up in front of the mirror primping. The rest rooms didn't even need toilets for

49

most of the girls, she thought, just mirrors on all four walls.

Sara pushed into one of the stalls. A rest room to her was strictly utilitarian. She listened to the buzz of the voices.

"And he said . . ."

"And I said . . ."

"Am I zipped all the way? It feels loose."

"How do I look?"

When Sara came out she walked in front of the mirror. She looked at herself, side face, front face, the other side. She raised her hand and pushed at her hair. She licked her lips and rubbed them with her little finger. The girls probably were too dumb to know she was mocking them.

"I didn't know you went with Sammy Carlisle."

Sara heard Sammy's name and looked around.

"Pardon?" she said.

"I didn't know you went with Sammy Carlisle," the girl repeated.

"Oh, we're just good friends." Sara tried to interpret as the other girls looked at each other and mumbled.

"Lucky" and "I saw him buy her ticket," were words that came through clearly.

She cocked her head and let her facial muscles find the places they had been when Sammy admired her smile.

"We're just good friends," she said again.

She was glad to get into fresher air. It couldn't be good for you to breathe all that stuff. She smiled at what they had said. They thought she went with Sammy. Dated! Sara laughed. Sammy was just Sammy.

She settled next to Sammy and told him in whispers.

"Hmmm?" he asked through a mouthful of popcorn. "Ohhh," he said when he finally heard her. "That could be very helpful. To both of us."

"What do you mean?"

"Sara Jane, you are naïve. Don't you know that there are certain girls who will be more interested in me if they think I'm taken? The same goes for you."

"I don't understand."

His words were indistinct as he pushed another handful of popcorn into his mouth. "If a boy thinks you like him, he will be more interested if he thinks you don't."

"Huh?" said Sara Jane.

"Shhh!" someone behind them said.

Sammy flapped his hand in dismissal and pointed to the screen. Sara tore the wrapper on her Necco Wafers and put one on her tongue. She liked to keep them in her mouth until they crumbled into sweet powder. Tally liked Necco Wafers, too. Sara thrust the thought from her mind and studied the names on the credits as the picture began.

During the movie Sammy's words came to her. So, she outran Gifford and told him to shut up and now he was interested in her because he had thought she liked him and now he thought she didn't!

And if you wore two different shoes people thought you were being initiated into a club and somehow that made them look upon you more favorably.

Further, if you went to the movies with a friend and that friend happened to be of the opposite sex, you were thought to be going together.

And then there was Tally, who always came when she was called, except once. Tears sprang to Sara's eyes. Embarrassed, she glanced quickly to see if Sammy had noticed. The movie seemed to have his full attention.

If she could get inside the skins of the movie people for a while, maybe her own skin could have a rest. She slid down into the seat and put another Necco Wafer on her tongue.

7

THEY CAME OUT of the movie giggling, moving along with
the flow of the crowd. Sammy knew almost everyone.
Two boys fell in with them.

Sara saw Kay with her friend Jean and waved. Out on
the sidewalk Sara stepped up to walk with them. Somehow
she would have to tell Kay about Tally.

Sammy and his two friends walked behind them. One
of the boys started making sly remarks and soon all three
were, even Sammy. One of the boys Sara didn't know at
all. The largest boy was John something-or-other. He was
on the football team.

"There's one each," Jean grinned mischievously. "I'll
take the one in the green shirt."

"I'll take Sammy," Kay said.

"That leaves Johnny Football for you," they both said to Sara.

"Not me," Sara said. They all laughed.

Jean looked over her shoulder at the boys.

"Hi there, big boy," she said in a teasing way, batting her eyelashes for emphasis.

"And hello, big girl," the boy in the green shirt said, lowering his voice and trying to sound sexy. He moved up on the sidewalk and pushed in between Kay and Jean.

Kay and Jean looked at each other and giggled. Kay half turned and began a conversation with Sammy. Sara looked back helplessly at the boy named John. She was being crowded off the sidewalk and John was now walking by himself. The steps she took while glancing back almost plunged her into a telephone pole. In the second it took her to sidestep, she was behind the others and Johnny Football was beside her. Panicky, she looked around for a way out of the situation.

"I don't bite," John said, sliding his arm through hers with planned casualness. "Honest I don't."

"But do you scratch?" Sara asked looking down at his arm and then back at him.

"Not that, either," he smiled. Not knowing what to do with her arm, she left it. The couples ahead were arm in arm, too. Sara took a deep breath. Maybe this was the time to learn how to relax with a boy who wasn't just a buddy.

"You're on the football team, aren't you?" She surprised herself by taking the initiative. Football, at least, she knew how to talk about.

"Yes, I am. Do you go to the games?"

"I wouldn't miss one. What's your number?" She knew numbers whether she knew names and faces or not.

"Thirty-four."

"Oh, yes. Johnny Dutton, defensive left tackle. You

surely can knock a hole in that line," she said with genuine admiration. She cringed inside at how phony she thought she sounded, like Kay saying "Another day, another dollar." But Johnny didn't seem to notice.

Sara wondered if he knew that she could probably block and tackle as well as he.

On Monday morning she saw John at school.

"Hi, Sara," he spoke loudly and waved across the moving heads in the hallway. "See you later," he called. Sara was impressed. For all her awkward feelings about yesterday, maybe those were the right tactics after all. Kay said that a boy likes to know you are interested.

Kay's conclusion was the opposite of what Sammy had said. But her show of interest in Johnny Football had gotten her farther than her lack of showing interest had gotten with Gifford Proctor.

She searched the halls for John between every class. She didn't want him to pass by unnoticed. But she didn't see him until after school.

In the mash of bodies after the last bell she saw him approaching. He beamed when he saw her and in spite of the lug of books he touched her shoulder as they passed.

"Hi, Sara."

Her heart jumped a little. Sammy yesterday and Johnny Dutton today. He wouldn't have exactly been her choice, if she could have chosen, but he was all right. She guessed she would just have to learn to be light and flirtatious, like Kay and her friends.

The next day she saw John twice during the day and he spoke enthusiastically. Once he doubled back and walked her to her class.

In the after-school crush they passed again. This time, too, he reached out to pat her shoulder, but his aim was a little low and his touch almost brushed her breast.

Sara swallowed hard. Surely it was accidental. She avoided Kay and kicked a stone all the way home. You are a prude, she lectured herself. Of course he didn't do it on purpose, especially in a crowded hallway with so many people around. No matter how many excuses she swallowed, the lump of doubt would not go down.

When the last bell rang again the next day, Sara was nervous. She forced herself to smile in greeting. As he approached, she sidestepped. He automatically made up the distance, reached out and touched her breast. The smile froze on her face. She kept her legs moving and allowed herself to be pushed along in the throng. She didn't look back to see if he was looking back.

Tears gathered on her lower eyelids. She blinked them away.

Again she avoided Kay. And again she kicked a stone home.

How could she tell Kay what had happened with her first attempt at flirtation? Kick. Kay was the one who had gotten her into it in the first place.

No. She hated it when people blamed others for their own actions. She had gotten herself into it by trying to act the way someone else acted. Coy looks and remarks might work fine for Kay, but Sara was not Kay. Kick. She had to learn to be herself, to trust herself.

Finding a new route from her last class to her locker was impossible. The only other way to go would be to walk around the end of the band room to the middle walkway behind the school. And what if she ran into John at the rear of the band room, with no one else around. Sara was frightened, no matter how she told herself that John wouldn't really try anything.

She kicked the stone down the hill and into the rock garden. She plunked her books on her bed and slipped into shorts. This was the time she missed Tally the most.

55

In hasty, smooth motions she walked to her tree, grabbed a branch, and swung up. The tree had leafed out since last week and it now hid her away from the eyes of the world.

Sara watched in silence as Kay came down Tarleton Terrace, knocked on Sara's door and, finally, walked back up the hill. Sara felt a little guilty. She just had to be by herself. A whole school day of pasting on a pleasant face and acting cordial was enough. Some days it was all she could do to keep breathing.

Miss Prissy Parmalee Dickerson came home, stepping daintily and looking across the street toward Sara's. Probably looking for someone to chase inside to study history. Sara smirked.

Then came Sammy. He would know to look for her in the tree. He would give her away and laugh about it.

Sammy walked up to the tree and leaned against it, musing, not looking up at Sara.

"Sara, are you hiding?"

"As a matter of fact, I am." Sara spoke sharply, not sure that he meant to leave her alone.

"Anything I can help with?" he inquired, still not looking up. He was cleaning his fingernails with his penknife.

"I guess not," Sara said.

"Well, let me know if I can help." He went up to the door and carried out a farce of knocking. He walked away when no one answered.

Bless your heart, Sammy Carlisle. Warm astonishment swept her. It was so rare that anyone really understood.

She braced herself for seeing John the next afternoon. She had made up her mind. If he merely passed, she would also merely pass. But if he made a pass at her—if he reached out a hand to her—she was, if it was in her power, going to knock him flat.

She made sure her books were nestled firmly in her left

arm. She didn't want them to go sailing helter-skelter and have to stop and gather them. She was hoping that he had finished with his fondle-Sara game. She tensed when she saw him coming.

Foot in front of foot, she made herself step steadily in spite of the trembles. She was near him now. He was smiling.

"Hi, Sara," Johnny said, just as though he'd been anxiously waiting to see her all day. Well, if he had really wanted to he could have seen her other times. And Alexander Graham Bell had invented the telephone. She saw John's arm leave his side and still she told herself it could be a mistake.

The hand extended, ready to pat her shoulder. But even though they were getting closer to one another rather than farther apart, the hand fell short of her shoulder and brushed across the front of her.

Sara's hand swung back, then landed resoundingly on John's jaw, partly on the face and partly on the neck. She hadn't realized how thick necked he was. The face and neck were as one and the smack was solid.

All movement in the hustle and bustle of the hallway came to a gasping halt. Except for Sara. She wended her way among the statues and kept her pace. She didn't look back; she heard the shocked silence lapse into murmurs.

Kay came running to her at the locker.

"Why did you do that?" Kay's dark-rimmed blue eyes flashed with excitement.

"I'll tell you—later." Sara was as out of breath as if she had run up a mountain.

Someone else came running up, and someone else.

"Did you slap Johnny Dutton?"

"Why?"

"Suppose," Sara said, "that you ask him." Her chin began to quiver and the tears that welled seemed to be starting down the inside of her nose. She sniffed. A sharp pain crawled up the back of her neck.

"What did he do to you?" Kay asked defensively. Kay looked as though she was ready to find him and slap him again.

"Later." Sara was blindly fumbling around in her locker, stalling for time, keeping her head almost inside the locker. At least Kay understood that John had done something.

"Just take your time. I'll let you know when everyone has cleared out."

When they left school, a clump or two of students were still milling around. There was a round of buzzing as Kay and Sara walked by. Sara kept her eyes straight forward, ignoring as much as she could.

"Whatever he got, you can bet he deserved it!" Kay announced firmly to the onlookers.

When Kay learned what had happened she was even more incensed. She spouted and sputtered and said what more Sara should have done to him.

"You should have kicked him!"

"What?"

"You know. Right between the legs. Nothing hurts a boy more."

"Really?"

"Sara, don't you know anything?"

"I wouldn't want to really hurt him."

"Well, if you're really in trouble with a boy or a man, that's the thing to do. With your foot or your knee. And hard." Kay demonstrated in the air.

Before supper Sammy came over.

"You mean your hand isn't still red?" He picked up her right hand and examined her palm. He moved it up in a simulated, slow motion slap against his own cheek.

"Sara, that was great. It just made my day. John's face was still red when practice was over."

"Oh," Sara moaned. If she had thought of spring practice, she wouldn't have done it. She shuddered, thinking of Johnny Football's embarrassment.

"Your entire hand print. Every finger! Boy, did the guys give him a razzing. And the coach!"

"Oh," Sara said again. She had felt the brunt of embarrassment too many times not to feel John's hurt. And the coach. What would he say to her now?

"What happened?" Sammy asked. In between his comments he was expelling the Sammy snicker.

"Didn't he tell you?" Sara asked.

"He didn't say anything. He just looked murderous. Some of the guys saw it happen and told it around, but nobody knows why."

"Well, you'll have to ask John."

"Ah, come on, Sara. You've got to tell me." He pressed his hands together and tilted his head, imploring. "Aren't we friends?"

"He got fresh."

Silence.

"He what?"

"You heard me, I speak perfectly plain English."

Sammy pointed his finger in her face. The guffaw started as a low rumble and roared upward. He grabbed his stomach and bent over.

"I'm glad I could give you a good laugh," Sara said tonelessly.

"Aw, Sara." Sammy came up, smothering his laughter.

"I suppose the whole school is laughing?"

Sammy opened his mouth, then closed it. She could see him searching for a lie and not finding it.

"You're right about that," he said in a minute. His eyes were laughing even if his mouth wasn't.

"The whole school!" Sara shuddered. She could never go back. How could she face everyone. And the coach, how could she take his teasing?

"But not at *you*," Sammy said. "They're laughing at John, not you."

Sara pressed her hands to the sides of her face. She wondered if she should apologize to John. But he owed *her* an apology. Apologies wouldn't save either of them from the humiliation.

At supper she shoved her food around on her plate, watching the abstract designs it formed.

"What's the matter, Sara Jane?" her mother asked.

Sara concentrated on the particular green of broccoli.

"I know what's the matter," Lowe said sourly.

Here we go, she thought. Lowe wouldn't give her the benefit of the doubt for anything. She was interested in hearing his version.

"She gets mad at this guy at school so she balls up her fist and socks him in the jaw. In front of everyone. My sister!" He hissed the word "sister."

Sara stared at Lowe. Mrs. Chambers looked down, embarrassed.

"Did you really?" Donnie asked, excited. Sara's chin started quivering again. She pressed her lips together and held the insides of them between her teeth. She placed her napkin beside her plate and left the table.

"I guess she did," Donnie said proudly.

"Sara, you didn't excuse yourself," her mother said.

"What do you expect?" said Lowe.

Sara kicked off her shoes and lay on her stomach on the bed. Everything she did turned into a mess. So, she didn't sock him. Sock or slap, she had clobbered him with all her strength. What if it was his first fumbling attempt at flirting, too? She doubted it, but it was possible. And anyway, was retaliation for his freshness worth humiliating herself before the whole school? She shuddered at the thought of defending her action by telling people why she had hit him.

She wasn't well known at school, but she would be now. In her fantasies she sometimes painted herself popular, graceful, and charming, someone everybody would notice. But not like this.

She stood in front of the mirror. Her mother, with high hopes, had installed a full length mirror. Sara swung her foot, tempted to kick the mirror. Seven years bad luck. So what.

Why would anyone even want to be fresh with you, she thought. Her breasts were small mounds. They barely made a dot in her blouse. Thirty-two A. Hardly worth touching. Certainly not worth a scandal. That was it. The whole episode was a joke, to mock her.

All she had was muscles, including one in her head. What had it got her to stop playing football? It hadn't gotten her Gifford Proctor. Her mother hadn't even noticed. She should have kept on playing and been killed in the crush. That would at least have solved her problems.

8

SHE was met with a barrage of questions before she was inside the school building. People she hardly knew kept asking,

"What happened between you and Johnny Dutton?"

Sara held herself straight and tall.

"I suggest you ask him." She was pleased that her voice came through calmly. No quavering, no venom.

Kay had picked and pestered all the way to school.

"I'd tell them exactly what happened," Kay advised. Sara relied on all the strength of the friendship between them to persuade Kay not to interfere.

"You'll have to ask him," she answered whenever she was asked for the story behind the slap.

"But he won't talk about it."

"And neither will I."

There was surcease in biology class. Everyone was too involved with frogs to razz Sara about Johnny Dutton. It was the long awaited, or dreaded, day to dissect frogs.

Sara had looked forward to it with great anticipation. If she was going to be a vet, she would be doing all kinds of surgery. This frog would be her first.

Sammy dangled his dead frog by a hind leg and elbowed Sara in the ribs.

"Do you think she'll let me roast the legs over the Bunsen burner?" He licked his lips and rubbed his stomach. "Hmmm, frog legs!"

Sara laughed only to be rid of him. An ignored Sammy became a persistent pest. She didn't like having Sammy next to her in class. He always tried to force her into horseplay and she was serious about her schoolwork. Especially today. He didn't, however, even mention Johnny Dutton.

She was a little nervous about making that first incision. She was afraid of finding some sign that she was not really suited for a medical career. She pinned her specimen securely to the dissecting pan. They had made their pans yesterday by melting beeswax and paraffin together.

Carefully, she stroked the tip of the blade across the tender skin of the belly. Perfect. And it was easy. She smiled and looked up to see how the others were doing.

". . . and I'm not going to do it." Jean Jones, Kay's friend, was talking to the teacher. Sara made a face. Somebody was always squeamish.

"What's that all about?" Sara questioned Sammy, nodding toward Jean and the teacher.

"She doesn't see why we have to use twenty-five frogs just because twenty-five people are in the class," Sammy whispered.

"She just doesn't want to do it," Sara said.

"I can study someone else's frog," Jean was saying.

63

"Dissecting a frog is a requirement for this course," the teacher said.

Sara bent over her work. She poked around the intestines, then proudly removed a tiny kidney.

"But I can do my diagrams and my microscopic studies without killing another frog." At this, Sara almost laughed. The frogs were dead already, steeped in formaldehyde.

"I'm not going to be a doctor or a nurse or anything in medicine or science," Jean continued.

Sara raised her eyebrows and looked up. Jean had a point. Why should so many frogs be sacrificed just so a bunch of tenth graders could learn the anatomy of a frog or prove they have strong stomachs? Actually, the whole class could study from one frog. Sara was glad she had her own frog, but, then, she was going to be a vet. It would be important to all her future patients that she knew what she was doing. Feeling sure of herself and not letting herself be overcome with second thoughts, she approached Jean and the teacher.

"Couldn't Jean watch me and do her work from my frog?" Sara asked, careful not to wave the scalpel while she talked. She was going to separate and label all the parts, but that wasn't required. All you had to do was identify and diagram all the parts.

A look of relief swept Jean's face. Jean reached out to touch Sara's arm but quickly drew back when she saw the scalpel.

"Otherwise, I'll just have to fail," Jean said.

"Don't you think it would be all right?" Sara asked. "The formaldehyde will keep any extra frogs until next year."

A debate was taking place on the teacher's face. She twisted her mouth and rolled her eyes. Sara stared at the scalpel. If she looked at the teacher, or at Jean, she would laugh. The teacher looked like a certain television comedian who did impersonations. He twisted his mouth and rolled his eyes no matter whom he was trying to imitate.

"It wouldn't be fair to the rest of the class," she said finally. "There are others here who would also rather not dissect a frog."

Sara looked around. Everyone else seemed to have begun.

"Can't we ask them if they mind?" Sara asked. "And see if any of them would prefer to work from someone else's frog?"

The teacher mused again, but at least she didn't make faces.

"Class," she said loudly, clapping her hands for attention. The room was already quiet. Heads lifted and turned toward the front of the room.

"Jean Jones is refusing to dissect a frog," she began. "Apparently her reasons are not those of squeamishness —" There were snickers. "—but in deference to the frog." Laughter.

"Poor little guy."

"I'm sorry little buddy." A few crooning voices crossed the room.

The teacher clapped sharply.

"Sara has offered to let Jean study from her frog, but I didn't think it would be fair to the rest of the class. I know others of you . . ."

"Sure."

"Let her go ahead."

"It's okay by me."

"Ain't nobody looking at my frog." That was Sammy. He hovered over his dissecting pan, blocking the view. Sara knew he was only kidding, teasing. Still, she wanted to kick him.

"Well, I suppose you may work from Sara's frog," the teacher said reluctantly. "Since no one minds. But your work must be excellent. And," she raised her voice to the class, "if any others of you wish, you may team up."

"Goody!" Jean shrieked. "Thank you." Jean followed Sara back to the table. Sammy already had several parts out of his frog. Sara looked around. Some students looked a little pale, but no one seemed to be taking up the offer to team up.

"You see, I have already removed one part." Sara pointed to the small organ lying away from the rest of the frog in the dissecting pan. "Do you know what it is?" Jean shook her head and searched the diagram in the book.

Piece by piece Sara dismantled the frog. Her book study had been valuable. She identified every organ without any difficulty. She forgot that Jean was looking over her shoulder. She was assisting Dr. Montini. No, she was in her own lab. Her mind was far removed from Johnny Dutton and the school-wide scandal.

The bell ending biology class also ended her peace. It was back to noncommittal answers and the struggle to be calm.

She dreaded seeing the coach in the gym. She couldn't ignore him. He was her mentor and a big tease.

"There's my girl. But I must be losing my touch. I thought I had convinced you to come out for spring practice."

There it was. There was his opening.

"I think I've retired." Sara tried to relax into her usual camaraderie. "I don't want them knowing the real reason, but they're getting too blasted strong."

"Ah, ha." He laughed. "Well, girls work out with weights, too, you know. Especially these days."

"Oh, I'm strong enough," she said, bulging her bicep.

"I'll say," he said, touching her knot-hard muscle.

"But it's a different kind of strength. Some of them are

turning into tanks." She stopped abruptly. Deftly, she had moved him away from the inevitable subject. Now, by mentioning tanks, she had come back to the starting point. Johnny Dutton was the most solid tank on the football team. The coach didn't miss it.

"Speaking of tanks," he said. "Do you need to tell me about yesterday?"

There it was, but gently, with no needle points. Why had she been so worried. Sure, he teased her, but he never made fun of her. She realized, suddenly, why she liked him so much. He liked her. And he liked her the way she was. He didn't make fun of her for playing football or for not playing football. He had not tried to talk her around to bookkeeping the day she told him she wanted to be a veterinarian.

"No." She moved her head with the word.

"If you ever want to, you know where to find me." He made her smile. He had made everything easy. And, finally, she was on her way home.

Norman, however, the neighborhood twirp, gored her with everything, after first making sure that his path for retreat was clear, of course. He wouldn't say "boo" to a goose on even terms.

"Well, if it isn't the K.O. Cutey," he greeted her as she came by his house on the way downhill from walking Kay halfway home. "St. George, slayer of football dragons." He was perched on the brick wall that partially enclosed his front porch. He could quickly swing his legs over to the porch and run into the house to his mommy.

Something about Norman raised Sara's hackles on sight. She had gained great satisfaction on several occasions by grabbing him and beating him silly. The desire was strong in her now, but he was safe. She scarcely looked at him as she walked by.

67

Emboldened, he called after her in a loud voice.

"Look at the tough girl go. Whatsa matter, turning chicken?"

Sara alternately scraped her upper and lower lip with her teeth. There were a number of offenses, any one of which was reason enough to want to smash Norman. Right now she wanted to give him all of her suppressed rages of the day.

Her mind began planning moves. Fancy him sitting there so smug and smart-alecky, swinging his legs! She could go around to the back of Sammy's house and come up behind Norman's house, then down the far side by the lot. She bet she could sneak up on him and grab his legs and yank him down from his sassy perch, if only he would sit there long enough.

She opened the front door and almost called Tally. It was such a habit. Tally had been her afternoon companion. She slipped quickly into some jeans. She flipped her dress over a chair and pulled on a sweatshirt as she moved through the house toward the kitchen door.

She checked to be sure that Norman hadn't come around to the back, then started to cross Sammy's backyard.

"Sara Jane," someone called in a loud whisper. "What are you up to now?"

Dave Kellerman was looking at her from his window.

"Oh, hi, Mr. Kellerman." Sara waved and kept moving.

"There goes that Mister, again," he said. "You make me feel like an old man. Come on in for a few minutes! And please call me Dave." He nodded his head toward the door and before she could decide what to do he was there, holding wide the screen door.

Oh, flitter, she thought. But she went over. He led her into the large sunny kitchen. Mrs. Kellerman was already pouring Sara a glass of tea.

"I think she was stalking that Norman guy." Dave Kellerman winked at Sara as he spoke to his wife. Sara fell apart.

"You," she said, "are a blasted mind reader!" Her inside self became her outside self with the Kellermans. It wasn't just that they were so nice, which they were. But, even more important, they were unattached to anyone or anything else in Sara's life. She didn't feel the need to cross-hatch herself with defenses.

"You just have that certain look in your eyes when you're going after Norman. What did he do this time?"

"Well, he . . ." She trailed off and then began again, telling them about Johnny Football and how she had maintained a cool exterior in the face of all the assaulting questions.

"You handled it with dignity," Mrs. Kellerman said.

Dignity? Me? She thought of how she had been today, calm in a crisis. She hadn't supposed it was dignity. She was pleased, but her pleasure pushed up a tiny fence, even with the Kellermans.

"Yeah, well . . ." she rushed on and expressed her anger with Norman before dignity could creep all over her.

"My, my," said Dave Kellerman. This time he winked at his wife. "I thought we might have to give Sara some growing up lessons, but I guess she's giving them to herself."

Sara put a bland smile on her mouth while her mind played badminton. Growing up lessons, being herself lessons.

"Yes," she blurted, "that's just what I need." She said it. They were the Kellermans, she could say it to them.

"Why do you think so, Sara?" Mrs. Kellerman asked softly. "You seem fine to me."

"But you said . . . He said that he'd thought about . . ." She faded again. Why did they back off? Where was she?

69

Why couldn't she make herself remain visible? Why did she keep disappearing inside herself? She forced it.

"Because I don't know how to be myself," she said quickly, running over the tears she was afraid might come. "I'm clunky."

"Sara," Mrs. Kellerman said. "You've got to learn to let yourself be, that's all. When you are with us, you are just fine. You are you. You are Sara Chambers, with or without the Jane."

"But out there," Dave took over, "out there you have all kinds of masks, being rough, being tough . . ."

"Crawling on my belly like a reptile," Sara interrupted. She shook her head and laughed. "Never mind, it's just this saying we have. 'He's rough, he's tough, and he crawls on his belly like a reptile.' It doesn't make any sense."

Both Kellermans laughed.

"You're all right, Sara," Mr. K. said. "You're really all right."

"Yes. Sometimes I am." She moved toward the door. They had pinned her in a dissecting pan and removed something, she wasn't sure what. But she felt better for it. She wanted to leave, go into the world, while the mood was still on her.

"Let me know when you are ready to give me my next lesson," she said. She walked up the driveway feeling a little glowy, a little confident. She thought about calling Kay, she felt like talking. It would be better, though, in person, this first real sharing. She'd go over.

She didn't even see Norman until she was almost out of the yard. He was coming down the sidewalk and he began a sliding sidestep when he saw Sara.

I will not let him make me angry, she vowed. I will not hit him. I am not, basically, a violent person. Norman kept his eye on her and just looking at him made her seethe.

70

Involuntarily, she balled her hand into a fist and began to raise it.

Behind Norman, she saw Giff emerge from the court-yard across the street. Her conscience slapped her hand and it dropped to her side.

But Norman's reflexes were already in motion. He lashed out in defense and landed a sharp knuckle on her mouth. Instead of rage she felt an immense calm. Her own hand, instead of flailing out at Norman, went to her mouth.

Norman fancy-danced around her, licking his thumb and flicking it on the tip of his nose. Over Norman's shoulder she saw Giff come running. Her knight in a velour shirt. Giff cuffed Norman on the shoulder and spun him around.

"Where do you come from, hitting a girl like that?"

Norman blubbered and sputtered as though it was just sinking into him that Sara hadn't hit back. Giff didn't give Norman a chance for explanations. Giff put a hand to Norman's back and shoved.

"You get on down the road, or up the road, wherever you were going and don't let me ever see you hit a girl again." Norman tucked his tail between his legs and moved.

"Are you all right?" Giff touched Sara's chin ever so gently.

"I think so." She moved her hand so Giff could see her lip. She licked out with her tongue and tasted the warm, salty blood.

"You need some ice on it," Giff said. "That guy is a jerk." With his arm around her shoulder he guided her to her door. She felt a warm rush of caring, enough to make her float.

She wanted to hold this moment forever, but there's

71

just so long you can stand at your door with your lip bleeding. Licking at her lip, she turned away from his holding.

"Thank you," she said. He was gone almost before she said it. Behind him he left the feeling that he was just doing his duty. She went in dreamily, just the same.

9

THE ringing telephone woke her. She winced when she
rolled over and looked at the clock. It was almost nine.
She wiggled herself into a comfortable position and closed
her eyes for another doze.

Her mother knocked and opened the door a crack.

"Telephone for you," she said. "It's Bill Sluker."

"Bill Sluker? What does he want so early in the morning?" Bill Sluker was the son of one of her mother's
friends.

Her mother smiled. "I guess you better talk to him and
find out."

Sara pulled the covers around herself and sat up. She
stretched her arms and legs as she walked into the hall.

"Sara Jane, this is Bill Sluker. Am I calling too early?"

"For Saturday morning? Yes." Sara couldn't imagine

73

why he was calling. She realized she didn't sound very cordial. "How have you been?"

She hadn't seen Bill since the Christmas holidays when he and his mother had dropped by to see Sara and Mrs. Chambers. She couldn't say that she had missed him—or even thought about him.

"The Braves are in town and I happened to pick up a couple of tickets for tonight and wondered if you'd like to go to the game with me."

Sara frowned. Braves, yes. Bill Sluker, no. She remembered him in his bathing suit at his family's pool last summer, diving under the water and coming up between her legs, hoisting her out of the water on his shoulders.

"Gee, I don't know," she stammered and stalled. She was fully aware that she was being asked for her first date. But weren't you supposed to be asked a few days in advance?

"I'll have to ask my mother," she said.

"I cleared it with her already," Bill said. Sara looked toward her mother's bedroom. Why had her mother put her in this trap?

"I'd better ask anyway. Just a minute." She lay the receiver on the telephone table and grimaced to herself. Here she was, ready to start dating boys and when she had the chance she wanted to back out. But she had hoped for a better start than Johnny Football or Bill Sluker.

"Well?" Her mother smiled when Sara came into the bedroom.

"He's waiting for my answer. Did you accept for me?"

"Now, honey. He just asked my permission. He knows you're only fifteen and may not be dating much yet. You're not upset, are you? After all, Bill Sluker. He's not just anybody." Her mother's smile was oozing.

No, Sara thought. He's not just anybody. He's the boy

74

who likes body contact sports—with me. Not to mention that his parents have money.

"You are going, aren't you? A Braves game. With your love for sports, I think it is a lovely way to begin dating."

Sara shrugged. She didn't want her mother to know what really bothered her about Bill, and she couldn't think of an excuse. She tried to think of a reason and, failing that, she went to the phone and accepted the date.

As soon as she hung up she dialed Kay's number. She picked the phone up from the table and stretched the cord to its length, placing it just inside the bathroom door. She went inside and closed the door.

"I hate to wake a sleeping beauty," Sara told Kay. "But it's happened. I've been asked for a date."

"Ohh," Kay squealed with delight. "Who is it?"

"Bill Sluker. He's a friend of the family."

"When?"

"Tonight. To the ball game. I really wish I had time to think about it."

"About what?"

"Whether I want to go or not."

"Think about it? Sara, you don't string a boy along while you think about it. You either accept or refuse. Besides, to a baseball game! What's to think about?"

"Well, he's sort of a creep."

"Oh. What kind of a creep?"

"Nothing I can really name. Maybe he's not a creep. But he gives me the creeps. He's good looking, though not really handsome. He's always been very nice. A little too nice, maybe. His family has a lot of money. He's got his own car, a convertible."

"And your mother will let you go?"

"With Bill she will. She thinks he's great."

"Sara, go and enjoy yourself. I dated a boy I thought

75

was a creep. I only went with him not to hurt his feelings. And he turned out to be so much fun."

Sara didn't want to tell Kay what made her feel creepy, how Bill Sluker kept coming up between her legs and wouldn't quit. She had been on Sammy's shoulders plenty of times, playing water battle, and it wasn't the same. Instead of trying to be the winner of the game, she felt Bill let them be knocked over. She got the distinct impression that the sooner they were knocked over the sooner Bill could lift her again.

". . . you go with a boy and maybe you will meet other interesting people." Kay was still talking. "At the very least, you can practice talking with a boy you don't care about to make it easier to talk with one you do care about."

Sara survived the day by pretending the date was with Giff. She kept thinking she would call Bill and break the date. Ah, Bill, something has come up . . . But she could never think of what. She manufactured funerals for fictitious aunts, uncles, and cousins. She put herself on restriction, for imaginary misdemeanors. She thought of having to go to her dad's with no way to get out of it. But she didn't call Bill.

It's a Braves game, a Braves game, she repeated to herself all afternoon and while she was dressing. When Bill knocked on the front door, Sara wouldn't come out of her room.

"Sara Jane, get the door, darling," she heard her mother call. Sara poked her head out of the door and pointed and mouthed, You get it!

Mrs. Chambers opened the door and greeted Bill. Sara heard them chatting. She sat on her bed and wished herself glued to it. She couldn't go out with a mattress stuck to her fanny. There was no way out of the situation but to go. She opened the door.

When they went out, the convertible top was down.

"Will it be too windy?" Bill asked.

"No, it's great." It really was. She liked having the breeze around her. The ride, at least, she would enjoy. And the game. And even Bill Sluker's company, she hoped.

As they curved around the Capitol on the expressway, the last of the afternoon sun glinted on the gold dome.

"Don't you love the gold on the dome?" she said to Bill. Every time she saw it she felt a new thrill, like a bolt of gold thrusting down inside her.

"Hmm?" Bill asked.

"The gold on the dome of the Capitol," she said.

"Oh, yeah. What about it?"

"I like it a lot," she said, only because it was mannerly to answer. Her enthusiasm for the conversation waned. "Don't you?" She twisted to look back as they passed.

"Yeah, I guess so," he said. Obviously, he'd never thought about it one way or the other. Maybe he'd never even noticed.

"You do know there is gold on the dome, don't you?"

"Mmmm," he grunted, nodding affirmatively.

Sara straightened in her seat and watched as they crept into the parking lot. There was a unity of movement as everyone streamed toward the stadium. Bill led the way to seats that were low and expensive.

"These okay?" Bill asked. She smiled, toying with the idea of saying "No." She preferred to sit higher and have a better view of the field. But the tickets were numbered and paid for, they had to be okay.

Bill hailed the popcorn vendor. Playfully, he fed her some popcorn. She tried not to recoil.

She wanted a scorecard and didn't know how to ask him for it. She fingered her purse. She could pretend to go to the rest room and buy a scorecard. No, that was cowardly. She rehearsed. Could I please have a scorecard? Probably she would stutter and stammer—uh, uh, uh.

Why was she so nervous? What was so frightening about asking for a scorecard? She tried to turn him into David Kellerman. Sure. The straightforward approach.

"A scorecard," she blurted the next time her mouth was empty. "Could, uh, we have a scorecard?"

"A scorecard?" He looked surprised.

"Yeah, you know, a program. One of those things that lists the players."

"Sure." He hunched his shoulders as if wondering what she wanted one for. But he was willing to please her—or impress her. He parked his popcorn with her and took the remnants of his orange drink and hot dog, which he had purchased in the meantime. He shuffled his way among the crowd.

He returned with the scorecard just in time for the announcement of the starting lineups. Opening the booklet to the center, she fumbled through her purse for a pencil and quickly listed the names.

"May I ask what you are doing?" Bill matched her hunched over position to be on eye level.

"The starting lineup. Don't you keep a scorecard at a ball game? You can't tell the players without a program." She cocked her head and grinned at him, pleased with her own witty lightness.

The first pitch was hit for a line-drive to shortstop. The shortstop snared it for the out. Sara bounced up and down and cheered loudly. She marked the scorecard accordingly. The awkwardness was gone. She was at a ball game and hardly aware of Bill Sluker.

Bill excused himself and went below and reappeared with more drinks. Sara looked at him and blinked. She had a big appetite herself, but she had barely finished the other

78

drink and the hot dog. She took the new drink and watched the game over the rim of the cup.

By the end of the game she had lost track of the drinks, candy bars, and other junk Bill had brought to her. She was so absorbed in the game she didn't notice when he left until he was back pushing something else into her hands. Once, he brought friends of his and introduced them to her. And once he brought her a pennant. She shrieked her pleasure as he handed it to her in the middle of a double-play.

At the end of the game, he guided her through the throng. He kept his hand at her elbow, maintaining contact. She liked having him there, protecting, caring. She felt the warm rush of response that she had felt with Gifford yesterday. She smiled and he squeezed her elbow.

In the car he reached out to her.

"You'll be warmer over here." He patted the seat between them.

"Oh, I'm fine, thank you." Sara forced some spirit into her voice and smiled again, trying to place all the facial muscles in the right places. She sat sideways, leaning partly against the back of the seat and partly against the door. She was glad her mother had given them orders to come straight home.

When Bill stopped in front of her house Sara had a premonition against lingering in the car. She opened the door on her side which gave Bill nothing to do but get out and go around the car to her side.

He held her hand as they walked up to the porch. His fingers intertwined with hers. She was uncomfortable, physically and mentally. There seemed to be such intimacy in the fingers.

"I certainly had a wonderful time," he said. "How about next week?"

Sara panicked. She had used all her resources just to get through tonight. She wasn't ready for this—dating, or Bill Sluker, she didn't know which.

"What about next week?" She played dumb.

"Going out with me," he said.

"Oh," she said. "Doing what?"

"There are lots of things we could do," he said.

"Well, you think of something and call me." He was very close to her and she was nervous. Her hand grappled behind her for the doorknob and turned it.

"It was a great game," she said. "Thanks for asking me." She summoned her shrinking muscles and pushed the door, backed in and closed it.

"Sara Jane?" she heard him through the door. Leaning against the door, she pretended she had already walked away and could not hear him.

"Is that you, Sara Jane?" her mother called. Sara put her fingers to her lips. Mrs. Chambers frowned, questioningly, walked over to the door and snapped off the porch light.

"Is he gone?" Sara whispered.

"Why, yes, he's just getting into the car." They heard the whirr of the motor. "Was it that bad?"

Sara waved her pennant.

"Rah, rah, rah," she said blandly. "He knows how to spend money."

"Well, he's got it to spend and he has liked you for a long time."

"He has?" Sara was surprised.

"Why do you think he got together all those swimming parties last year? Didn't you have a good time?"

So, all the innuendoes in the water play were not figments of her imagination.

"I had a very nice time, really," Sara said. It was what her mother wanted to hear. And she *had* had a good time—the game, the feeling walking back to the car with him at her elbow. His attitudes, not his actions, bothered her. He seemed so possessive, so aggressive. And the "if-you-accept-a-date-with-me-I-own-you" thing. Sara couldn't explain it. What had he done, really, but be nice?

"Well, dear, I'm glad you had a good time." Her mother smiled as mother to child, as though Sara had enjoyed a red lollipop. Sara returned the smile and went to her room.

10

KAY, of course, wanted to hear every microscopic detail of Sara's date with Bill. Sara went over to her friend's house on Sunday afternoon after Kay had returned from the weekend father trip.

"Did you have a good time with Bill?" Kay asked. "Do you like him better than you thought you would? Did he kiss you?"

"On the first date?"

"Oh, Sara, don't you know anything?"

"No, he didn't kiss me," Sara said firmly.

"Did he try to? Did he try anything else?"

"Boys don't try things with me," Sara said. "I speak from vast experience," she added, giggling.

"Who are you trying to kid?" Kay asked. "This is me,

Kay, remember? I'm the one who knows why you slapped Johnny Dutton."

"Can't you ever forget that?" Sara asked. "That was different."

"How so? He's a boy, isn't he?"

"Don't make categories," Sara said. "I hate that. All boys are like this, all girls are like that."

"Well, I've never known of a boy yet who won't see what he can get away with."

Sara thought of her earlier feeling that she had possibly provoked the incident with Johnny Dutton, she had purposely put on an act.

"I don't believe it," she said.

"You speak from your vast experience?" Kay asked, laughing. Sara laughed, too.

"What you need," Kay said, taking a book off the shelf, "is a good book." Kay tossed the book at Sara.

"What's this?" Sara caught it in mid-air and glanced at the title.

"It tells it like it is," Kay said.

"Like what?"

"Like the birds and the bees and the boys and the girls."

"Like what?" Sara repeated.

Kay leaned over and retrieved the book from Sara. "The pages aren't glued together, you know." Kay thumbed through the pages.

"Well," she sighed, closing the book and tapping it against her knee. "You should read the whole thing. It's written by a minister and is very moral but also very straightforward and detailed."

"I know all about those things," Sara said, embarrassed. It certainly wasn't anything she went around talking about. Or reading books about, either.

Kay rolled her eyes. "You need to read this book more

than anyone I know. You're beginning to have dates and I don't think you understand the feelings in your own body. Didn't you want him to kiss you? Haven't you ever wanted a boy to kiss you? Don't you ever get that, uh, feeling?"

"I don't know what you mean." Sara shrugged and wanted fervently to drop the subject. She remembered the warmth and comfort of Bill at her elbow, before he ruined it. And the rush of tenderness for Giff as he expressed concern over her lip. Were these feelings related to what Kay was talking about? Was she at the beginning of the kinds of relationships which, in the future, would develop into love?

"There's this certain feeling, you know," Kay said. "It's the same feeling you have when you, you know, when you get married." Kay's voice trailed off. "You've never had that feeling?"

Sara shook her head, unable to make such an admission out loud.

Kay put the book in Sara's lap. "Haven't you ever thought about a boy that way?"

"No!" Sara exclaimed. If she denied ever having had the feeling, perhaps it was that she had not recognized it. She knew for certain, however, that she had not thought about it in general, much less in particular. Maybe she was retarded in her development, a late bloomer, or else Kay was too advanced. Sara didn't know which.

"Well, you know, Sara—" Kay laughed, tapping the book—"the stork didn't bring you." Sara sneered, tucking her mouth in at one corner.

"I know all about that. It's just that I never . . . I never thought of it about myself."

"You sure better start thinking," Kay said. "I mean, you can't wait until your wedding day before you let the idea cross your mind. Things like this, you have to think about them a few years to let your ideas and feelings develop."

"I know. That would be a shock, wouldn't it?" It jarred her just thinking about not thinking about it until her wedding day. "I guess I thought it was sinful to even think about it," she went on, "if I even thought about it that much. Have you ever thought that way about a boy, a particular boy?"

"I do sometimes, but it doesn't seem to work out in my mind. The way I figure is that when I feel I will enjoy letting a certain boy do that with me, then I guess I'll be in love. I'll think, that's the one I want to be the father of my children."

"You don't think you'd ever feel that way about anyone else?"

"Now, that's something I never thought about," Kay said.

"Well, you must, or at least some people must, from what I hear."

That night Sara dreamed the same dream over and over. She was lying in a big double bed and Bill Sluker walked into the room and over to the bed. He lifted one leg, as if to get into bed. The dream flicked back to Bill walking into the room. He walked toward her repeatedly. Sara awoke and wondered how many times she had dreamed it. She couldn't recall what Bill had on, pajamas, clothes, or nothing.

She was repelled by the dream. Whoever it would eventually be in reality, she was sure it would not be Bill Sluker. She went back to sleep and didn't dream about Bill any more.

11

BILL's next telephone call took Sara by surprise. She had just about thought him out of existence, and if he didn't exist, he couldn't call.

But there he was, sounding quite alive at the other end of the line.

"I'd like you to go with me to our school dance Friday night," he said.

"I'm sorry, Bill, but we're having a dance that same night." Sara was glad to have a ready reason.

"Do you have a date?"

Trapped. She wasn't expecting him to do other than accept her statement.

"No." She spoke before she had time to think up a lie.

"Well, why don't we go to your dance for a while and then go to mine?"

The kindness of the suggestion startled her. How could she refuse when he was interested in her and had been really very nice. It wasn't his fault she had dreamed about him.

"But I have to be home so early." She stalled for time, seeking a more solid excuse.

"So? What's time? I'd rather spend a short time with you than a long time with someone else. We'll go to your dance from eight to nine and to mine from nine to ten. I could have you home by ten-thirty if you have to be home that soon."

Sara's face was doing all sorts of contortions. She was glad he couldn't see her.

"I'll have to ask my mother."

Sara's mother, of course, said, "Yes, since it's Bill." The door of the trap closed. But Mother, Sara didn't say, I don't want to go. Can't you make an excuse for me?

Sara had never had a formal dress. In fact, she only went shopping if forced. She hated trying on things. She hated it when the salesperson pulled back the edge of the curtain and said, "How are we doing?"

Mrs. Chambers dragged Sara on a round of dress shops and department stores. Reluctantly, Sara donned formal after formal in shop after shop.

"Now this one looks lovely on you," her mother said.

"It's not comfortable," Sara said, slipping it off immediately.

"You have to give it a chance," her mother said.

"I have to be comfortable," Sara insisted. She had rejected dresses by the rackful. If she was going to go through with this, the dress would have to be just right. Otherwise, she would break the date for sure. Uncle Somebody would die or at least become gravely ill.

At last one dress went on smoothly and fell into comfortable contours across her breasts and hips. As Sara turned to look at herself from all angles, she caught the look of hope in her mother's eye.

The dress was white eyelet, sleeveless, with a modest V-neckline. A slash of Kelly green satin circled the waist and trailed prettily down the back.

"You look so lovely," her mother said. "You're becoming quite a young lady."

Sara smiled at herself and at her mother. It was odd to Sara that such a simple thing as a date, a dance, and a pretty dress could make her mother feel at peace with Sara.

"Next thing we know you'll be forgetting about being a veterinarian and start thinking about what you really want to be."

"Mother!" Sara croaked. Oh, why were people's equations so lopsided. "I am going to be a veterinarian."

"I know." Mother was all patience and condescension. "That's what you think now. But you'll grow up."

Sara sputtered to herself as her mother helped raise the dress over Sara's head.

"Mother, haven't you heard of individuality? I don't fit into your idea of me. I am not you. I am not anyone but me. I am an original. I wasn't cut from a pattern—like this dress. Sara struggled to put her half-formed thought into words.

She shoved the dress into her mother's hand. All of the glimmer vanished from her mother's face.

"I thought you liked it." Her mother sounded defeated.

"I do. I want the dress." Sara let the exasperation slide into her voice. "Buy the dress. I just want you to know that that dress doesn't have a thing to do with changing my ambitions. It may change my appearance, but it doesn't change me. I'm still here."

Later, Kay came over to see the dress. Kay was more excited than Sara.

"What time is he coming for you? How long are you staying at our dance? What kind of flowers is he bringing?" Kay plied her with questions.

"I don't know if he's bringing flowers."

"Of course he will. Things haven't changed that much." Kay held the dress in front of Sara and stepped back to take a look. "Cymbidiums would look pretty with your dress."

"What are they?"

"Small orchids. They're greenish and bronzy."

They sounded awful to Sara. But Kay was right. Bill brought flowers. Not cymbidiums, small orchids, but two huge purple orchids with dark velvety throats. They were gorgeous. As Sara cooed over the flowers, Bill preened.

"Let's see, Sara Jane." Mother hovered, holding the corsage first to her shoulder, then to her wrist.

"You're not going to pin them there," Sara protested in mock seriousness. The pretentiousness of the flowers became obvious as they sought a place to put them. Finally, her mother pinned them at the left shoulder.

"You look lovely. You look marvelous," Bill said too many times. He ushered her to the car and punched a button. The top began rising from the back like the Loch Ness monster from the sea.

"Why are you doing that?" she asked. She liked having the top down.

"So you won't get windblown."

Sensible, but she would have liked to have the wind beating rhythms on her face. Anything to annihilate her queasy feelings. Why had she mentioned her school dance? She had never been to one before, nor cared to go. The next best thing to being back home would be to go where no one knew her.

Eagle-eyed Kay saw them right away and glided over to be introduced to Bill. At least Bill was nice looking, no one would have to feel sorry for her on that account.

"Oooo, he's handsome," Kay whispered to Sara as the two boys shook hands. Kay looked darling, as usual. Her black hair was piled on top of her head and her pale eyes sparkled out from between dark lashes. Kay's dress was red with white gores inset in the skirt.

The two big orchids seemed to bulge from Sara's shoulder. If she moved her head the slightest bit to the left her chin brushed the flowers. She felt like she was on exhibit. Everyone, it seemed, was buzzing over to speak to her. But when she looked around, no one was gaping at her. It was only Kay and Jean and Sammy and friends from the neighborhood.

Bill gave just the right measure of attentiveness to her friends and moved Sara out onto the dance floor. Sara moved with the beat, but she wasn't enjoying herself.

Sammy danced with her and didn't make one crack. She kept wishing for Giff, but Giff was inseparable from a red-haired girl. A matched set. Bill danced with Kay and Kay's date danced with Sara. Sara absorbed it all with a remote numbness.

"Now you are really launched," Kay whispered to her as she and Bill prepared to leave. But it wasn't fun to be launched if you weren't ready to sail.

In the car Bill patted the space between them.

"Come on, move over a little," he urged. Ho, hum. Sara felt she'd been over this ground before. She took her post against the seat back and the door.

"It's cold over here." He was persuasive and just the right amount of handsome when he smiled. She didn't want to be a clod. She took advantage of the fullness of her dress and straightened herself in the passenger seat, just a little to Bill's side.

"Well," he smiled and sighed. "That's a little better." His emphasis was on "little." She was still some distance from him, but the skirt of her dress touched his knee. He seemed very self-assured.

She began to feel pretty. If people couldn't say that she was with a creep, they wouldn't say that he was, either. Her confidence was building by the time they reached his dance.

"You remember John and Susan from the ball game," Bill said, introducing her. Sara smiled and nodded.

"Nice to see you again," she lied. She didn't remember meeting anyone at the ball game.

"I'm surprised you remember," the boy said. John. His name is John. "You were so involved in the game." She searched her mind, but all she could remember was cheering and having Bill poke food into her hands.

She was pleased they remembered her.

She tried to imprint John and Susan on her brain so that she would recognize them if she saw them again in a few minutes. She must make herself pay more attention to people. The way to have a friend is to be one, she thought.

She nodded and smiled as Bill introduced her to others. She caught herself memorizing Susan's dress as Susan moved away. Bill eased her onto the dance floor.

She saw herself at school, in the rush between classes. She didn't look for Giff, she looked for his shirt! No wonder she didn't know many people. They changed clothes every day!

Susan and John were dancing nearby. Sara forced her attention away from their clothes and concentrated on their faces. Susan, blue eyes, medium brown hair, a special shape to the lips. John, dark complexion, bushy eyebrows, slightly downthrust nose.

The small band was very good and the dance floor was lively. Sara enjoyed her relative anonymity. She felt free

91

here where no one knew her. Suddenly she realized Bill was staring at her and smiling.

"What are you smiling at?" she asked.

"It's wonderful to see the way you enjoy yourself," he said. She smiled. She felt the rightness of being herself and being liked for it. She was herself, the way she was with the Kellermans and with the coach. It was a special way of feeling, fitting inside your own skin.

They crossed the parking lot swinging their joined hands. He wasn't squeezing his fingers in between her fingers, just comfortable, hand in hand.

"Can we have the top down?" she asked.

"We can have the top down if you will sit close to me," he said. She smiled and slid over. There was a temptation to kiss his cheek. Except for the flowers, he hadn't been at all show-offy. She was pleased by his sweetness.

With the press of a button, the top of the car was swallowed. The wonder of life was in the air, caressing her nostrils and blowing her hair around her head. Leaning her head against the back of the seat, she relaxed, satisfied, content. In spite of herself she had had a wonderful time.

"Home already?" she said when he stopped. "It's been such a lovely evening."

"Home already," he echoed, sorrowfully. He turned toward her then. His right arm stretched out and moved around her shoulder, pressing her to him. The orchids began to flatten between them.

"Oh, Bill," she said quickly, "my flowers."

"I bought them. I can crush them if I want." He laughed. He continued his pressure and moved his left arm around to encircle her.

"But these are my first flowers," she said, touching them. Deftly, as though he'd done it many times before, he pulled the corsage pin out of the orchids and set the flowers on the dash.

"How's that?" he grinned and slid over to her. Something about his determination frightened her. To her, it seemed quite possible to kiss without smashing the orchids. She remembered her dream, when he kept coming toward her.

"Uh. I really must go in now," she said. She reached behind her for the door handle, but, more quickly, he pressed his finger down on the lock button. She could not twist around far enough to pull up the button.

"What's the harm in a kiss?" he said.

"No harm," she said. "It's just that . . ." He kept moving in. His face was very close to hers.

"Bill, stop it!" She had hoped to extract herself from the situation without having to be so blunt. She stretched herself into a primly erect position that put her chin above his head. For a moment she thought he was going to let his head fall and nestle at her breast. He sat back, abruptly, and pounded his fists on the rim of the steering wheel.

"Why?" he asked her. "Why?"

"Why what?"

"Will you just tell me why, after I have spent money for two dances, and brought you flowers, you can't thank me with a kiss?"

"I gave you the tickets for my school dance," she reminded him. "Besides, I don't sell my kisses for two dance tickets and a corsage. I thought you wanted my company."

Sara surprised herself. She usually couldn't think of things to say in a tight situation. She felt she had expressed herself very well. It was certainly true. Her kisses were not to be purchased by an expensive evening. No matter how old-fashioned it was, she wanted her first kiss to be special and Bill Sluker just wasn't.

93

"You're not getting out of this car until you kiss me," he said.

"You mean it's that mechanical? After what we have just said to one another you would still get pleasure out of a kiss?"

"Yes."

"Well, then, I'm just as sorry as I can be." He was fully on his side of the car and she on hers. She lifted the button latch, opened the door, and swiftly exited. Even so, he lunged so quickly that he almost caught her. He lay across the seat with his arms outstretched.

"Shall I walk up by myself or would you like to accompany me to keep up your image with my mother?" She waited a moment for his answer. If at all possible she was going to manage the situation without resorting to the methods she used on Johnny Football.

She could practically see the fire darting from his eyes. Slowly, he sat up and slid out his side of the car. The door closed with a resounding slam. Sara pushed the door on her side with her foot. He gripped her elbow more firmly than necessary and stalked her up to the porch.

"I'm sorry it turned out this way," Sara said, trying to make some sort of amends. "It really was such a lovely evening until just a few minutes ago." She was attempting to read his mind. He was struggling to say something—or not to say something.

All in one motion he put his hands on her shoulders and kissed her solidly on the lips.

"There," he said with vengeance.

"Did you really enjoy that?" Sara asked. He was already turning and striding down the walk. Sara opened the door and went in. Again she leaned against the front door. Her eyes were stinging. My first kiss, my first dance, my first flowers. There was nothing special about it.

"My flowers!" It made her smile. The flowers were on

the dashboard of his car. "He got the kiss and the flowers, too!"

Surprisingly, Bill called again and again. Not knowing what to say in the face of such persistence, Sara finally asked her mother for advice.

"Just say you have other plans," Mrs. Chambers said. "You don't have to tell him if your plans are to wash your hair or to listen to the radio."

On this basis Sara steadfastly refused Bill's invitations.

12

THE SCHOOL BAND was practicing for a parade and Sara automatically fell in step with the music as she approached the school grounds. The blue sky was an escape hatch for troublesome things and Sara felt good.

The music entered more fully into Sara's consciousness and she looked up. The band sounded terrible. Her eyes marched up and down the rows searching for Kay. Kay was very musical, she played the flute and the piano and she sang.

Sara spotted Kay and she also spotted the reason for the sour sounds.

Marching with the band was a short, stocky black and white dog. Not only was he marching, but he was joining in the music with a baleful howl. Most of the band members were getting pitiful sounds from their instruments as they attempted to blow while giggling.

The band director, baton still waving, sidled between the marching students and tried to shoo the dog away. Nothing doing. This dog was having fun. The director used his foot as an incentive. The mutt kept marching and howling.

Laughing, Sara wove her way through the band members and took the dog by the scruff of the neck and dragged him away.

"That your dog?" the director asked angrily.

"No, sir," she answered.

"Well, keep him away from here!"

Sara dragged the mutt around to the front of the school and let him go. He was an ugly old thing.

"I'm surprised he didn't take your hand off," someone said.

"Whose dog is he?" Sara asked.

"Nobody's. He's just a stray. He's been hanging around here for several years, but no one has ever been able to put a hand on him."

"How does he eat?"

"Some people put scraps out for him, but mostly he knocks over garbage cans."

"Aw, he's too small to knock over a garbage can."

"You should see him. He may be small but he's a strong little rascal."

Sara could grant that he was strong. He wasn't more than a foot tall, but he was heavy and muscular and had been hard to drag. But he hadn't tried to bite her. He hadn't even growled.

"The dog pound has orders to shoot him on sight."

"Shoot? You mean with darts?"

"Bullets. They've tried to catch him for two years. He's

a nuisance. Just the same, I'll hate the day I see him lying in the gutter."

Sara winced. She pictured the black and white heap, streaked with blood, lying in the gutter waiting for garbage pickup.

She walked around to the back of the school again and there he was already, his short little legs running to keep pace with the band. His moderately long muzzle was tilted upward and his mouth was opened roundly. She dragged him away again.

"That your dog?" the director asked again.

"Yes, sir," Sara answered.

"I thought you said it wasn't your dog." He was livid. "Don't you know there's a leash law? You keep him away from here!"

"Well, sir," she began, but the music had started again and the director couldn't hear her. She continued anyway, "He wasn't my dog, but he is now."

She left him in front of the school with orders "to stay" while she went inside to see Mrs. Wilkes.

"My dog followed me to school. May I have permission to take him home?"

"I don't see how, Sara Jane. After all, the bell . . ."

Unbidden, tears watered her eyes. She didn't really mean it. What did that little old dog mean to her, anyway.

"Well, all right, Sara Jane. Honestly, what am I going to do with you?" Mrs. Wilkes spoke with affection and Sara smiled. It seemed no one knew what to do with her— least of all herself.

"I don't see any need for you to be upset all day. How long will it take?"

"Thirty minutes," Sara lied. Well, if she rode her bicycle back maybe she could make it in thirty minutes.

Sara ran outside, but the scroungy hound was nowhere

to be seen. She ran around back to see if he had rejoined the band. The band was dispersing, and there was no dog.

"Have you seen that crazy dog?" she asked.

"He went that-a-way," someone said, laughing and pointing toward the street. Sara ran down the bank and looked up the street. There he waddled. His tail had a wide white plume that waved as he walked.

I'll call him Flag, she thought.

She hurried to catch up with him. He looked over his shoulder and broke into a trot. She knew she wouldn't catch him, running. She stopped.

She squatted down on the sidewalk and whistled and rubbed her fingers. He turned and looked at her, then ran again.

Okay, you stinking mongrel. Get yourself shot and thrown into the gutter! To her surprise, she was crying. Somehow this mangy mongrel was her.

She returned to school and went to the rest room to splash her face with cold water. Her darned eyes. They stayed red for such a long time after she cried. She opened them wide so they could air-dry. Finally a look in the mirror showed her eyes clear and she went to class.

"Did you get your dog home all right?" Mrs. Wilkes asked as she walked in.

"Yes, thank you," Sara lied. No telling what Mrs. Wilkes would say if she knew Sara didn't even have a dog. She settled into her desk and looked at the blackboard for her assignment. They were to write a description of one of the several subjects listed.

She had a hard time keeping her mind on what she was doing. English composition was usually her easiest subject. In Miss Parmalee Dickerson's class, where even total attention could draw fire, she was still distracted.

"I see Miss Sara Jane Chambers is not really with us

today," Miss Dickerson commented sarcastically. "I'm sure she'd quite rather be home climbing trees."

A few snickers rippled through the room and Sara felt herself turning red. She sucked her bottom lip in between her teeth and closed her eyes. When she closed her eyes Miss Dickerson got all mixed up with that stupid little mutt. She saw him lying in the gutter and he turned into Tally, cold and still.

After school Kay promptly pronounced Sara crazy.

"I'm sorry. I've got piano, so I can't help you look for a phantom dog. He could be anywhere by now."

But Sara spotted him down a side street. She wished she had some meat, but if she stopped to get some now she might lose him.

She approached him casually, as though she were just passing by. He moved over on the sidewalk for her to pass. As she went by she stopped.

"Hello, poochie," she said in a beckoning voice. "Sweet doggie. Nice boy." He gazed up at her, blinking. He didn't move when she stooped. Still talking, she reached out very slowly. He was within her reach if only he would let her touch him.

He wiggled his rump and backed up a few steps. At least he was not running. Sara waddled a few more steps and kept coaxing. Step by step they worked themselves halfway down the block. She glanced at her watch; she couldn't spend all afternoon.

"Well, good-by, old boy. Take care of yourself." She wanted to pat him on the head but, of course, he would not allow it. She stamped her foot and told him, "Shoo! Go to wherever it is you hide, and hide."

The next day she was almost frightened to go to school. She had visions of seeing the dog in a heap, with the arrogant independence knocked out of him forever.

Sara armed herself with Tally's collar and leash and

some hamburger meat. She wrapped the meat and stuffed it into a Thermos to keep it from spoiling.

The mutt wasn't in any gutter she passed, nor was he anywhere else, not even following the band. But after school she found him. He wasn't any more interested in her with the meat than he had been interested in her without it. He stood, just beyond her reach, appraising her with his solemn brown eyes.

Tired of stooping, she sat down. She refrained from reaching out to him, so he didn't back away. She pushed some meat toward him and removed her hand. He didn't even lower his nose for a sniff.

"You spoiled brat!" she said to him.

She had made up her mind to be patient. But she began to wonder if he couldn't outdo her when it came to patience. She toyed with the idea of lassoing his head with the leash. He would struggle, she knew, but she had confidence in her ability to calm him.

She began to flop the leash around in her lap to get him used to the motion. He did not bolt; he kept standing, staring. She eased toward him and he hunched, ready to move. Sara looped the leash through the handle. She leaned quickly and dropped the loop over his head and pulled the end to tighten the noose.

He bucked and jerked and snarled and snapped. A horse couldn't have been stronger or wilder. Someone had said he was vicious and now she was seeing it. Just as no amount of coaxing had made him come to her, now no amount of coaxing would calm him down.

He frightened her. Unable to contain her terror, she dropped her end of the leash and he ran bucking and snapping down the street.

Sara, usually unflappable when it came to dealing with animals, was shaking. Well, that was that. It was a foolish thing to do. She had wasted fifty cents' worth of hamburger and now he had Tally's leash, too. She took a deep breath, held it as long as she could, and let it all blast out at once. She picked up her books and started home.

Her toe chose a rounded stone and connected squarely. She didn't know whether these stones were her friends or her enemies. Maybe both. She cupped the stone between her feet, curb-hopped, and kicked again.

No resident father. No understanding mother. No boyfriends. No one to share things with completely. Not even a dog. Self-pity settled on her like a cloud as she mechanically paced herself to kick the stone along.

For no reason that she knew of, she looked around. Half a block behind her, looking solemn and dragging the leash, was the mutt.

"Well, well, well," Sara said aloud. "Come on. Come along." She turned her back on him again and kept kicking the stone. Every few steps she looked over her shoulder. He was coming. He seemed to be telling her that he wanted to come but only in his own way and on his own terms. She reached that understanding with him.

Her mother was predictable. "Let him go and see if he runs home." Sara could not seem to get the idea across that he had no home. She had fed him and watered him and managed to pet him. She was sure he was hers.

In the morning he was gone.

That afternoon he followed her home from school again. He continued this procedure for several days before he decided to stay.

He was a mean old thing. Try as she might to call him Flag, he was just Mutt. When she took him to Dr. Montini for a checkup and shots, he almost took the doctor's arm off.

"You'd better break him of that," Dr. Montini said, quickly grabbing Mutt's muzzle.

"How do I do that?" She was patting Mutt, crooning softly to calm him down.

"Well, you get some heavy work gloves and smack him in the snoot. If you want to keep him, you'll have to settle him down. Right now I'd say he's a pretty rough playmate."

Mutt kept snarling and the doctor didn't release his grip.

"Well, you do as I say and he'll be fine. You're good with animals."

He injected Mutt with the rabies vaccine and pronounced him in good health. Sara scooped him off the table, then set him back. It was now or never to ask him that question. The worst he could say, she thought, is no. And that shouldn't kill me. She braced herself for a negative answer.

"Dr. Montini," she said. "You wouldn't happen to need some part-time help, would you?"

"Still wanting to be a vet, are you?" He smiled.

"Yes, sir. More than ever."

"It so happens I will need someone when school is out. My clean-up boy graduates from high school and is going straight to college. Are you interested?"

"Yes, sir!" Sara felt like clicking her heels and saluting.

"It's not glamorous work," he said.

"Oh, I know that."

"It's cleaning cages, mostly, and bathing dogs."

"That's okay." She was grinning and holding Mutt close. Dr. Montini grinned broadly.

"All right. I'll look for you the Monday after school is out. That will give George a week to train you before he leaves."

Again she took Mutt from the table. She backed out of Dr. Montini's office, smiling and repeating, "Thank you."

"And good luck with the mutt," he said.

On the way home Sara bought some heavy gloves. It would mean the difference between keeping him or not. Knowing that he could sense her fear and would react to it, she made up her mind not to be afraid. She settled down on the front porch and gave him a bone.

When he began to gnaw, she took the bone from him. He came at her like a tiger and she backhanded him across the muzzle. He snarled and snapped. She put her hands around his jaws.

"No, Mutt. No."

He jerked and snorted trying to free himself. She patted him with her free hand and praised him. When he settled, she returned the bone. As he started chewing, she took it from him again. Snarl, snort, gobble. He was at her again.

Summoning up willpower she didn't know she possessed, she ignored her fear. She desperately wanted this dog. He could never replace Tally, but somehow he had come alongside Tally in Sara's heart.

After repeating the process a number of times, the dog finally stood unhappily but quietly when she took his bone. They had reached a truce. Once more she returned his bone and this time she let him have it uninterrupted.

She circled his neck and nuzzled him. She had another dog. And she had a job, a real job helping a vet.

13

SARA hadn't been roller skating for a long time. So there were two reasons why she was a little apprehensive when her father planned a skating trip for them.

The other reason was Joyce, his new wife.

In the two years her dad had been remarried, Sara had only seen his wife at the apartment. Whatever outings they had, Father's Wife stayed behind. Sometimes Donnie had pleaded for "Mama-Joyce" to come along. So, now that she was coming, Donnie was more excited than usual. Lowe was as passive as ever.

Sara had never felt jealous of Joyce before, at least not that she recognized. She was surprised at her feelings of resentment about Joyce joining them. Joyce even had her own skates.

"I haven't really used them much in years," F.W. said. "But I used to love to skate."

Sara chewed the inside of her cheek. Maybe F.W. would fall and break her rear end. For all her skill in athletics, Sara had never been a fancy skater; jumps and twirls were not her style. It really bothered her that Joyce might outdo her on skates.

When she realized what she was thinking, Sara was a bit surprised with herself. She really didn't want to wish harm to anyone. But, giving in to her fantasy, she wished it anyway. "I used to love to skate," she mimicked in her mind, adding a high pitch that F.W.'s voice didn't really have.

An unwanted bubble rose to the surface of her thoughts. She tried to sit on it and keep it down. The knowledge popped and spattered all over her. Joyce had Sara's father and Sara did not.

Bringing the feeling to the surface did not make it disappear. Now that the thing had identity, it magnified her shame and hurt.

The skating rink was like a huge warehouse. The entrance was from a darkened side street. Sara felt as if she were sneaking into some illicit place.

She picked up a pair of skates at the rental window, went to a bench, and began loosening strings. Since F.W. hadn't had to wait for her skates, she already had one on. Sara scrambled at the strings. She wanted to beat F.W. onto the floor.

Before Sara had the strings tightened on the first skate, F.W. was rolling toward her.

"Can I help you?" F.W. reached for the second skate and began loosening the string.

Don't be nice. Sara pressed her lips together. Just don't be nice. She pulled the top of the laces and deftly tied them into a bow.

"That's okay, thanks. I'll be ready in a minute." She reached up and took the other skate from Joyce. To Sara's chagrin, F.W. sat down on the bench beside her. Sara yanked at the top of the skate and thrust her foot down into it. While she worked with the laces, Joyce made an attempt at conversation. Sara wished for Donnie. Donnie's specialty was naïvely filling in awkward gaps. But Donnie was a couple of benches away with their father. Lowe, naturally, was on a bench by himself.

"Have you skated recently?" Joyce asked.

"No." Sara answered. The word hung in the air, a blunt solitaire, lonely in spite of the whirling hubbub around them. There was the constant whirr of moving skates, the jumble of voices, and the music. Every now and then the announcer would coincide his voice with the lighted sign, "All Skate," he would say. Or "Couples Only."

"You do skate?" F.W.'s statement was a question.

"A little," Sara replied.

When she stood she felt steadier than she had thought she would. She rolled toward her father and Donnie with Joyce at her elbow.

"Go on out," Dad said. "We'll join you in a minute." He had his own skates on and was helping tighten the laces on Donnie's skates.

"Where's Lowe?" she asked. It was a dumb question. Since when did she care where Lowe was? Or he her?

"He's already on the floor."

F.W. touched her arm and started onto the floor. Sara recoiled inwardly at the touch but followed. She would not intentionally hurt Joyce's feelings by refusing to skate with her.

Her feet rolled smoothly beneath her and did not betray her uneasiness. Left, right, left, right, she roll-stepped around the rink. She noticed Joyce. Joyce was just plain old skating. Maybe she doesn't know any of that fancy stuff. Once around the rink and they paused for her father and Donnie to come on with them.

"Can you do some tricks?" Donnie asked Joyce.

"I used to do some. I don't even know if I can any more." Joyce was smiling. A snag of guilt pinched Sara. She was wishing calamities again.

"Maybe after while I'll see what I can still do, okay?" F.W. ruffled Donnie's hair.

The four of them glided onto the floor, Sara alongside Donnie and F.W. with Dad behind them. Donnie swung his arms and took long forced strides. In a moment he sped ahead of her. Sara put the "nix" on everyone and pretended she was alone. She let her body sway with the music. Flash thoughts flicked across her mind.

She and Kay ought to come skating sometime. They had good times together. Kay was becoming a truly good friend. Like Tally. Like Mutt. She smiled; Mutt was such an arrogant individual. Except for not being quite so possessive about his food, he still insisted on having things his way. She smiled about Mutt, then smiled about working with Dr. Montini. The knowledge made her glow.

She couldn't smile about Giff, though. In spite of the passing weeks, the sight of him still thrilled her with sadness. After his first little response to her apparent lack of interest, after his heroics with Norman, he had faded away. She saw less of him than of anyone in the neighborhood. Somewhere, like Lowe, he had his own detached life. With the red-haired girl, Sara guessed. Except for a few greetings in passing, Sara was totally excluded.

Someone nudged her arm.

"Get off the floor, stupid."

It was Lowe. The "Couples Only" light was on. He condescended to skate with her long enough to complete the circuit to where they could get off.

Dad and F.W. came skating by and a feeling of strangeness came over Sara. Dad's arm was around F.W.'s waist and she was leaning into him. On the curve their ankles crossed over in perfect symmetry. They were a pair, a couple, not just for this couples skate but for always.

"Will you skate with me?" Donnie had come up to her unnoticed. She shook her head. Disappointment spread across his face. She relented.

"All right. Okay." Just as they rolled onto the floor the "All Skate" came on and the music changed. Donnie streaked ahead of her and Sara followed him with her eyes.

Donnie caught up with Dad and F.W. who had ceased the leaning but were still skating side by side. Donnie came up alongside F.W., slipped his hand into hers, and looked up at her.

Sara could imagine the conversation. If there was going to be any fancy stuff, it would be now. F.W. looked at Dad and the two of them moved toward the center. Donnie glided to the side.

The center of the rink was reserved for those doing other than straight skating. Sara had been watching some skaters there as she circled the rink. Now she pretended not to watch.

F.W. was so darned graceful. She didn't look at all out of practice as Dad held her hand above her head and F.W. pirouetted. She did a few jumps and turns, then jumped and almost did a split before she landed in a smooth glide.

Dad held out his hands to her and they began dancing on skates. Dad stumbled, caught his balance, and laughed. He and F.W. beckoned to Donnie and the three of them joined the regular skaters.

Sara rolled off the floor and went to the rest room. She was sucking on her lips, trying to pull the sting out of her eyes. It was just possible that Dad and Joyce loved each other. Why couldn't she accept it? If he was miserable with her mother and not miserable with Joyce, why should she wish him back into his misery? She went into a booth, pushed the latch, and let the tears come.

A knock on the stall door startled her.

"Sara Jane? Are you all right?"

It was F.W. How had she known it was me? Sara looked down at her feet. She had on white socks and dirty white skates, just like dozens of other girls.

"I'm fine. I'll be out in a minute." She started fanning her eyes, trying to clear them so they wouldn't tell on her.

"Are you sure?" Joyce asked.

"Sometimes it just takes me a while," Sara answered. She saw F.W.'s feet under the door. Her skates were gleaming white and the laces were green and white plaid. They moved away.

Coming out of the rest room and back into the din was like turning the television volume up full blast. When you were in it you became immune to the noise, but the walls of the rest room had dimmed it. Dad came up to her and took her elbow.

"Girlie, when you have to leave, let someone know. We didn't know where you were."

"What could have happened?"

"I was looking for you when they had the 'Couples Only.'" A pang of joy and sorrow reverberated through her.

"You didn't skate with Joyce?"

"Well, I did when I couldn't find you. But I wanted to skate with you."

Sara went back out onto the floor, but she kept her eye on her dad and on the lighted sign. She sat out a rhumba and saw Lowe sitting it out also. Dad and Joyce and Donnie had their hands on each other's hips and were skating around one-two-three kick. It looked like fun, but Sara couldn't make herself join them even when F.W. and Dad called to her as they went by.

Then, he was beside her.

"There's a 'Couples' next, I think," he said. Her eye went to the light, which blinked from "Rhumba" to "Couples Only" as she looked.

"I don't skate too well with anyone," she said. "I need my arms for balance."

"I'll balance for both of us," he said. He put his arm around her waist and guided her to the floor. He moved with graceful sureness.

"Lean into me and match my steps," he said. It was hard for her to lean. She couldn't remember ever having had anyone put his arm around her like that. She was a little self-conscious.

"Lean," he said again. He jiggled her off-balance and she had to lean or fall. He gripped her firmly and she moved along with him. She relaxed and leaned and matched her step to his.

He was so solid and surefooted, she knew she would not land on the floor. Soon she had the joy of moving around the rink gracefully herself. It was over too soon and he was separating himself from her.

"See?" he said. "You did beautifully."

Donnie and F.W. were suddenly there. They had skated the "Couples Only" together and Sara hadn't even seen them. Lowe came sailing past, alone. Sara broke away from her father and started around the floor.

A newfound sense of security warmed her. Casually, she held her hands behind her. She swayed to the music and the hum of skates. Her mind flitted to Giff, as she thought of "Couples" skating. She was surprised to feel that he did not fit the rhythm. Bill Sluker? She shuddered. Johnny Football? Yuck. Well, that's all right, she thought, smiling. She could stand, or skate, on her own two feet.

She thought of her father. The patience and care he had shown in teaching her things, like skating and diving, was his way of showing his love. Why was she so afraid to show her own? That day in the apartment when he had wanted to talk, all she could do was ache inside and be flippant outside. He had needed her understanding just as she needed his. And she had shut him out.

The light flashed. "Last Skate, Rhumba." Sara looked around for the others. She gathered with Dad and F.W. and Donnie.

"Come on, Lowe," she called to him. She had been very effective at shutting people out. Lowe didn't respond.

They moved onto the floor with Dad in the lead, then F.W., then Sara and Donnie flying along behind. A-one-and-a-two-and-a-three, kick. One-and-two-and-three, kick. Sara began to laugh.

Letting go with one hand, she signaled to Lowe as they rolled past.

"Come on," she called, smiling and genuine. It was an evening for understanding. Lowe wasn't really a snob. He must be just as churned up inside as she was.

She remembered when they were younger. They had been friends. They had played marbles by the hour with the pattern of the living room rug for a ring. Once they removed all the books from the bookshelf and, using them as blocks, built a great fort.

"Come on," she called as they passed him again. She felt sorry for him now. She wished she knew how to help him release the things that bound him. He just sat, watching, giving no acknowledgment. She ached for him.

But she was having too much fun to hurt for long. So, be that way, then. You'll just have to help yourself.

She laughed as she went around the rink. A-one-and-a-two-and-a-three, kick!

14

SARA walked and talked with cheerful vitality. She felt good about herself. She even felt good about Miss Parmalee Dickerson.

"Do you know that poem about the good bear and the bad bear?" she asked Kay as they walked along to school. "The bad bear gets better and the good bear gets 'wuss!'"

Kay shook her head. The poem was from A. A. Milne's *Now We Are Six*, a book Sara had read to shreds.

"Well, I don't know who's getting 'wuss,' but I'm getting better."

Kay smiled. "What's put you in such a good mood?"

"Oh, lots of things. I have my outline finished."

"Your history outline?"

"Yup." Sara opened the edge of her notebook and

patted the title page. "Just think. I'm almost finished with Miss Dickerson!"

When she went to history class, she handed in the outline with a great sigh of relief. Sara watched Miss Dickerson as she placed the papers on the corner of the desk. Miss Dickerson didn't seem to notice. Flitter. Sara wanted Miss Dickerson to see that Sara Jane "Tree-climbing" Chambers had completed the long assignment and turned it in on time.

At the end of the period Miss Dickerson assigned homework. It was the last week of school, but Miss Dickerson kept you working right down to the wire. After announcing the homework assignment and without changing her voice tone or pattern, Miss Dickerson said, "Sara Jane Chambers please remain after class."

If Sara's attention had lapsed she would have missed it. The bell rang. Sara was tempted to walk out and pretend she hadn't heard. It couldn't be good news whenever Miss Dickerson wanted Sara. At least, it hadn't been all year.

She tried to conquer her feeling of foreboding. Hadn't she turned in her outline? Hadn't it been the very best job she could do, even surpassing her usual neatness? Maybe the stalemate was over. Perhaps Miss Dickerson wanted to compliment her for a job well done.

Sara forced a little life into herself as she approached the teacher's desk. She gripped her armload of books firmly.

"Yes, Miss Dickerson," she said brightly, adding a smile.

Miss Dickerson had Sara's outline in her hand. She didn't look up. She tossed the paper-clipped pages to the side of the desk nearest Sara.

"This is all wrong. It will have to be done over."

Sara was sure her ears must be deciphering the message incorrectly. She looked up at the ceiling, then shifted the position of her feet so that they would hold her more sturdily.

"Pardon me?" Sara questioned.

"I said," Miss Dickerson said, "that this outline will have to be done over. It is not acceptable." She patted the top of the work for emphasis.

"I don't understand," Sara said. She picked up the papers and flipped through them. Miss Dickerson hadn't even had time to look over it. The words on the page seemed to be moving around, trying to get into acceptable order.

"Will you please show me what is wrong so I will know what to do?" Sara tried to sound as polite as possible. She had to have this outline approved in order to pass.

"As I told you before," Miss Dickerson said as though it were just yesterday, "I do not teach English."

"How long do I have?" Sara asked, resigned. They had had six weeks to work on the outline. How could she possibly get it redone in a few days?

"Since it was due today, it will be overdue in any case. And," her tone of voice was so kind, so benevolent, "since this is the last week of school I obviously cannot give you any longer than Friday. Please turn it in before school so I can make out your report card."

Sara swallowed hard. Tuesday, Wednesday, Thursday. That was hardly enough time to recopy the material, much less make corrections, especially when she didn't even know what needed correcting.

Sara walked out of Miss Dickerson's room in a trance. The hall was quiet. The next period had already begun. Miss Dickerson's hammer had knocked out a big chink from the dam and Sara's finger was not big enough to plug up the hole. She went to the office.

"I'd like permission to go home," she said to the secretary. "I don't feel very well." On cue, her chin began to quiver and tears slipped through the dike. The secretary took her name and looked up her schedule. Sara took the pink "permission to leave school" slip and padded her way down the silent hall.

She was glad her feet knew the way. She was incapable of guiding them herself. They kept moving, one after the other, and occasionally, automatically, her toe kicked a stone. Without her conscious help, however, her feet did not repeatedly seek out the same stone and kick it all the way home.

She was moving so ploddingly that she almost fell down the cinder slope. The pebbles rolled under her foot and she skittered in a standing position. Sara didn't care if she fell. It might even feel good to have the gravel grind into her elbows. She would just lie where she landed and not move.

But she didn't fall. Her feet maneuvered the cinders automatically, too. As she started across the yard she saw Dave Kellerman going into his apartment with an armload of stuff. She stopped and waited until he was inside. She wasn't in the mood for any chitchat, not even from David Kellerman.

She fumbled around for the door key and finally managed to place it in the lock and turn it. Mutt was barking furiously somewhere within. She found him shut in the bathroom.

"My goodness. Have you been in there all day? Poor baby." She stooped and tried to pet him in between his jumping and continued barking. "Oh, come on now. It can't be that bad. You're out, now." Somehow in the rush of the morning Mutt had gotten shut in the bathroom. She ran back in her mind. She didn't recall doing it, but it had to be either she or Donnie. Mutt didn't follow her mother and Lowe. Unless Lowe did it for meanness.

Mutt trailed her to her room and when she fell across the bed, he jumped up on the bed beside her. He licked her face and nuzzled her hand and barked and whined. Sara moved her hand onto his back and rubbed him.

"Ah, we've both had a bad day." How could life be such a roller coaster? This morning had been so great. How could things turn upside down so quickly? Mutt lay down under her touch and they were both still. She fell asleep.

She awakened to a soft knocking at the door. It was Kay.

"How are you feeling?"

"Oh, I'm not sick. Not physically, that is." She told Kay about it.

"Well, come on and take a walk. It'll make you feel better." Kay was interested in a different boy, but a dog still made a good excuse for walking around wherever it was one might want to walk.

"I'd better not, since I left school sick. I'm quite sure that Miss Dickerson knows about it, through her mystic powers. What I don't need today is any more of Miss Dickerson."

"I wanted to tell you about an end-of-school spend-the-night party Jean is having Friday night. I told her you would come."

"Oh, you did, did you?"

"Yes, I did and you are. Can I take Mutt for a walk?"

"You can try, but I don't know if he'll walk for you." When Sara and Kay were together Mutt didn't seem to care which one of the girls held his leash. But Sara was right. When Kay snapped the leash to his collar, Mutt sat down on his short little bottom and refused to move his feet. Determinedly, Kay dragged him across the porch and bump-bump-bumped him down the stairs.

"He's a passive resister," Sara laughed. "You might as

well give up. All you'll do is sandpaper his rump." Sara called Mutt and he bounded to her as Kay let go of the leash.

"The stinker," Kay said.

Sara went in and thumbed through her outline. She studied the details. She could find nothing wrong with it.

"I will *not* do it over, Miss Parmalee Dickerson," Sara said stoutly. "You'll just have to fail me!" Sara had never had an "F" on her report card. In fact, it was rare that she had anything below a "B."

It would be just my luck to fail, and have to have her again next year. This thought made Sara reconsider the outline. She had had such a terrible time this year it would be horrible to have to go through it again.

She had periods after each number and letter. There were at least two subtopics under each roman numeral. The first letter in each topic and subtopic was capitalized. Sara just didn't know what else Miss Dickerson wanted. She had the feeling that Miss Dickerson hadn't even looked at the outline. Maybe I'll just fail you, Miss Parmalee Dickerson, she thought. Maybe I'll just take this outline and show it to the principal and tell her how I have been harassed. Perhaps you'll be the one in trouble, my dear Miss Dickerson.

She wandered out to the kitchen. In the dining room a buffet drawer was open. It was the one where her mother kept her sewing. Scraps of cloth were spilling out onto the floor.

"Donnie," Sara yelled. No answer. Sara denied a twinge that urged her to pick up the mess. She was tired of Donnie's continuous rummaging.

She popped two pieces of bread in the toaster and held her hands above it to feel the heat. With her toast she went to her nest.

The feathered branches clothed Sara with a little security. She tried to think, but her mind was blowing in the wind like the mimosa leaves.

Up the street some of the gang was playing ball. The sounds tempted Sara. She felt like joining them. Giff was part of the past. She drew herself up small when she saw Miss Dickerson drive up. A delivery truck was taking up space across the street and Miss Dickerson parked in front of Sara's house.

Miss Dickerson's mother was with her. The elderly lady was with Miss Dickerson often, but not always. Sara had decided that the old lady only lived with her daughter part of the time. The older woman looked as if she had walked right out of the "Whistler's Mother" picture, even to the white handkerchief and the white lace cuffs on the long black sleeves. She was, however, without the bonnet.

The teacher, her own age belied by her artificially colored blonde hair, rounded the car and opened the door for her mother. They were almost under Sara.

". . . don't think it's proper," the mother was saying in a nagging voice. Sara smiled. Miss Dickerson was getting it about something. Sara silently cheered the old woman on.

"Mother, I refuse to discuss it," Miss Dickerson replied. At the same time, she supported her mother's arm and assisted the exit from the car.

"Well, I will continue to discuss it, Parmalee, until you come to your senses and come home. I never thought a daughter of mine would live alone without any supervision whatsoever and . . ."

Sara snickered. Miss Dickerson must be forty or close to it. Sara didn't know why Miss Dickerson bleached her hair. If it was to make herself look younger, it didn't work. Maybe Miss Dickerson just liked blonde hair. Or maybe who knows, she did it to anger her bossy, conservative mother.

Sara wondered what hopes and dreams Miss Dickerson had for her life. She certainly didn't seem to enjoy teaching. Probably her mother thought teaching was proper for a lady, like living at home. Maybe she wanted to be a mountain climber, or even a vet, like Sara.

Sara thought about her blowouts with her own mother. Often, she had guilt feelings about them afterward. But, at least, her mother would never be like Miss Dickerson's.

Did Miss Dickerson have a boyfriend? She bet Miss Dickerson had gotten her own apartment with high hopes, anyway.

Now, thinking of Miss Dickerson made her sad instead of mad. Maybe she just picked on Sara when something else was bothering her, the way Sara sometimes lashed out at Donnie when she was mad or upset, even though it didn't have a thing to do with Donnie. Not that Donnie was such an angel. Sara had scars on her legs where Donnie had kicked her with his hard-toed shoes.

What would happen to Miss Dickerson if Sara complained to the principal and was taken seriously? Would Miss Dickerson lose her job? Perhaps she could talk to Miss "D." about the problem between them. No, Sara knew she could never make the words come out right. In her head she began composing a letter. "Dear Miss Dickerson. I would like to straighten out the misunderstanding that has been between us the whole year. I am very bad at talking, so I am writing you this note. You probably don't know it, but I am a very shy person and only have one or two friends. At the first of the year everything was changed around from last year. I was assigned to your homeroom and I didn't know any of the students in the room. I was so miserable. Please believe me, it would have upset me for the whole school year."

Ha! Sara snorted to herself. She had been upset for the whole school year anyway, but just in history, at least.

She agonized over the phrasing and struggled to complete the letter.

"It didn't have a thing to do with you. I didn't even know you. I just wanted to be in a homeroom with at least one person I knew. Mrs. Wilkes knew some of my problems, so she changed me. I realize now that it looked as though I was trying to get out of your room. It wasn't that at all. I was very selfish and was thinking only of myself. I didn't stop to think how you would feel."

She went inside and committed the note to paper.

15

SARA put the note to Miss Dickerson in a plain envelope and set it on her dresser. She was feeling better again. Those two bears! One gets better and the other gets "wuss." She even went to the kitchen to start dinner. When her mother came in she was hard at work.

"Sara Jane," her mother called to her now. "Come here a minute, please." Sara finished cutting the last potato and tore off a paper towel to wipe her hands.

"Sara Jane, dear, was this like this when you came home?" Her mother was in the dining room looking at the scraps of cloth. Sara could already hear the standard lecture: Don't just walk over a mess; whether it is yours or not, pick things up as you go from room to room. Sara had been up and down enough for one day.

"Not that I noticed," she lied. "Some of Donnie's messing, I guess."

"I don't think so," her mother said. Sara began bracing herself for the blame.

"How about this?" Mrs. Chambers crossed the room and pointed to the studio couch. Sara's room doubled as a guest room and when it was in use as such Sara slept in the dining room.

On the couch, now, was a large grocery bag on its side. A few things were spilling out of the bag. Apparently her mother had a list of accusations. Sara made a face and shrugged.

"He sure made a mess, didn't he?" She reached out to pick up the silverware that was lying on the couch away from the bag. Her mother touched her arm and stopped her.

"Don't touch it. Come here." They recrossed the room and her mother lifted the lid of the silverware chest. It was empty.

"If you think," Sara began her defense. What did her mother think Sara wanted with all that stuff?

"Calm down, Sara Jane. I don't want to frighten you, but I think we've had a burglar."

"What? Are you sure?"

"I am trying to be sure. Look." Her mother pointed to the hall. On the floor by the basement door were a couple of winter coats.

"Have you called the police?"

"Not yet. I wanted to be sure . . ."

"Oh, Mom. I just scream and yell. I don't wreck the joint."

"I know, but the way you are sometimes . . ."

"Oh, Mom." Sara cried and fell into her mother's arms to be held.

123

While they waited for the police they talked of nothing else.

"What I can't understand is why that dog didn't chew the burglar up. He even growls at me if I have to shake you awake. I thought he'd be a good watchdog. It's the only reason I let you keep him."

"Mother. Mutt was accidentally shut in the bathroom this morning. He was about to tear the door down when I came home. I thought it was because he'd been shut up all day."

Something blipped Sara's mind. It was a picture of Dave Kellerman entering his apartment with a pile of—what was it? She put the picture on stop action and examined it from where she had stood in the backyard, not wanting to be seen. He'd had an armful of clothing.

Sara felt sick. A sour taste filled her mouth and throat. Dave Kellerman. Oh, God! Dave Kellerman knew Mutt better than anyone but Sara and Sammy. He could easily have put Mutt in the bathroom.

"Did he go out through the basement?" Sara started for the hall.

"Wait, Sara Jane. Wait for the police."

The basement was just an earth dugout that housed the furnace. There was a never-used small door from the basement to the outside. It was concealed by bushes and came out by the driveways, the Chambers' and the Carlisles'.

Sara looked at her picture again. Dave Kellerman, now that she looked carefully, had been crossing the driveway rather than coming down it.

"You must have frightened the burglar off when you came home," her mother said. "Thank God he wasn't bold enough to stay."

Lowe came in from baseball practice just before the police arrived. Donnie appeared at the first sign of the police car. Mutt growled furiously and Sara shut him in her bedroom.

The officers opened the basement door to ascertain the escape route. Sure enough, there was a pair of Lowe's slacks on the bottom step.

"He left in a hurry," one officer said.

"My daughter came home from school early. He must have heard her key in the lock. Thank God." Mother squeezed her again.

The outside door was closed firmly, but unlocked.

"This is how he got out, but how did he get in? Are you absolutely sure this door was locked and bolted?"

He opened the door and they all came out through the bushes. Sara tried to keep her eyes away from the Kellerman apartment. If it had been Dave, she knew he hadn't been frightened by her key in the lock. Was it possible he had seen or heard her coming down the cinder bank?

She kept her back to the Kellermans'. Their kitchen window was just across the Carlisles' driveway. Mrs. Kellerman was pregnant. Did they need money that badly? They seemed to be doing okay financially. No, his being there had to be a coincidence; he wouldn't have done anything like this. But maybe he noticed something.

"I wonder if the Kellermans saw anything," she said.

"Who?" The two officers turned to her. Her mouth felt full of sand. She desperately needed a glass of water.

"I came in the back way," Sara said. "Mr. Kellerman was just coming home, going in his door." Even with this suggestion she felt she had turned him in. Why did she feel so certain? She had no proof, no proof at all.

Mother pointed to the Kellermans' door and also gave the Carlisles' name. The police wanted to inquire around the neighborhood to see if anyone had noticed anyone hanging around.

Sara's legs were wobbly. She barely made them rise high enough to get back up the stairs. Things refused to stay in focus. Everyone thought she was upset about what might have happened had the burglar still been in the house when she came in. Mother fixed her hot tea with milk. Even Lowe was solicitous.

"I didn't shut Mutt in the bathroom," Lowe said. "And from now on I will check every morning to make sure he is loose in the house."

When the officers returned, Dave Kellerman was with them. Sara felt like a guilty traitor. But Dave wasn't in custody. He was just present as a concerned neighbor. He bobbed about asking what he could do to help.

Mutt began to raise a wild ruckus. Since Mutt had growled at the policemen at first, his racket was attributed to their presence. Sara watched Dave. He never met her glance.

Had the officers told Dave that she had seen him "coming home"? Would he be naïve enough to think she wasn't suspicious? Or did he know that she knew? He gave no indication.

The officers left, assuring the Chambers that there was almost no chance that the burglar would come back. They had dusted for fingerprints but, of course, they had not fingerprinted those present, of whom Dave Kellerman was one.

"Just remember, I'll be right next door if you need anything." Dave oozed assurance as he left right behind the policemen.

As a matter of fact, Sara said silently to his back, there are a few things that we do need. Like the stuff you stole from us.

Sara looked at her mother. She could feel her mother's confident dependence on this hulk of an ex-marine, David

Kellerman. Yesterday, she would have had that same dependence herself.

In spite of the officers' assertion about the burglar's not returning, none of them wanted to sleep alone in their separate bedrooms. They helped each other drag mattresses to the living room. Lowe contributed his baseball bats as weapons. Donnie, with childish bravado, took a few practice swings. He was full of excitement and ready to knock off someone's head.

There was a family solidarity that hadn't been achieved in a long time. Warmth and family love bound them together. They all felt it, even Lowe.

In the morning, Donnie passed the news along to those who hadn't heard. For several days small-sized Sherlocks skulked around asking questions, seeking clues.

On Wednesday, Sammy glumly announced that the Kellermans were moving. Thursday, as Sara came down the hill from Kay's, she saw a U-Haul trailer in the Carlisles' driveway. At the bottom of the drive, Sammy bustled about, helping. Sara ignored the proceedings and hurried into the house.

She went to the kitchen and peeked out from behind the filmy curtains. The trailer was already loaded. Something inside her lurched.

Dave appeared, struggling with a big box. Boy Scout Sammy rushed to his aid. Somewhere in one of those boxes, Sara thought, are our things. Why else would they be moving so suddenly?

"What are you doing here?" Donnie surprised her, chugging into the kitchen and attacking the cookie jar. "I thought you'd be out there helping. I thought they were your friends."

What could she say to the super sleuth? In spite of herself, the sting of tears spread through her eyes.

"Oh, I get it," he said, nodding. Clutching a handful of cookies, he went as quickly as he had come. The next thing she knew he was outside by the U-Haul.

"Sara Jane's in there crying because you're moving," he announced loudly. He pointed to the kitchen window. She stepped back quickly. That little brat. That devil. She clenched her fists and dug her nails into her palms. She pictured them all gaping at the window.

She skittered into the dining room and peeped out of that window. The Kellermans were coming around the U-Haul to the car. Dave opened the car door for his wife. Instead of getting in, she stood there. They seemed to be talking seriously. Dave gestured, palms up, the universal symbol of helplessness or "I don't know." He shrugged one shoulder.

Mrs. Kellerman left him, then, and walked up the drive-way. Sara, feeling what was coming, closed her eyes and waited. Even so, the sound of the doorbell sent a series of shocks down her spine.

"Sara? Sara?" Mrs. Kellerman called out from the other side of the door. Sara gripped the back of a chair. She tried to make her own back as straight and hard as the chair back. Finally, she went to the door. Opening it just a crack, she peered out.

"Sara, I didn't want to leave without saying good-by." Sara, feeling foolish behind a protective barrier, opened the door wider. It was as though she was the criminal and by opening the door she was revealing herself.

She tried to force "I'm sorry you're moving" off her tongue. It was the correct thing to say. But she wasn't sorry. The Kellermans' presence next door was, somehow, a condemnation. She had opened herself completely to them. This sharing had meshed their lives so that Dave, by doing this thing, had involved her in it, too.

"It's always hard to say good-by to friends," Mrs. Kellerman said. "And sometimes, for special reasons, it's harder than others."

Mrs. Kellerman reached through the doorway and drew Sara into a quick, affectionate hug. Sara felt her own stiffness. What was Mrs. Kellerman saying? Is she saying that she knows? The words could mean anything.

"I was hoping to have you as a baby-sitter," the young woman said quickly. "You would be very reliable. As you know, everyone isn't." Now what does she mean by that?

"Good luck with the baby," Sara said, grateful for something to say that was genuine. "And with everything," she added.

Dave had pulled the car and trailer up to the front of the driveway. He drove far enough so that the corner of the trailer was between him and Sara. Sara wasn't sure whether she was relieved or sorry that she couldn't at least wave to him.

"Tell Dave I said good-by," Sara said as Mrs. Kellerman started off the porch toward the car.

Dave turned left on Tarleton Terrace, up the long hill. Sara didn't know, hadn't asked where they were going. If she didn't know, she couldn't possibly send anyone after them, even if she was tortured, even if she tortured herself. She wasn't sure whom she was protecting, Dave, Mrs. Kellerman, or herself. Perhaps all three of them, preserving what they had had.

She watched until the trailer disappeared under the tunnel of trees. She felt rather like a tunnel herself, hollow, empty. Her insides felt twisted all the way down.

For the first time since Monday, they all slept in their own beds that night. Sara missed the closeness.

16

ON FRIDAY Sara went to school early and placed the history outline and the note on Miss Dickerson's desk. As she came out of the room a boy spoke to her.

"Miss Dickerson certainly has been on your back," he said. "I know you're glad this year is over." Sara looked at him, vaguely recognizing him. He must be in her class.

She appraised him quickly, trying to study him and not his clothes. Yes, it seemed now that she remembered him. Medium height, sandy brown hair, green eyes. His nose was very pointed; she smiled when she noticed. She had smiled at just the right time.

Newly sympathetic toward Miss Dickerson, she said, "Yeah, well, it's a long story. I don't mind so much any more."

He looked at her in surprise. Sara was trying to make

him look more familiar. Was he in her class, or had he heard about Sara Chambers and Miss Dickerson? She really should pay more attention to people. She had sworn she would. By now she should have known everyone in her class.

"I don't think I could be that charitable," he smiled. He was very neat, almost too neat, but he lacked the aura of a sissy.

"I wasn't at all charitable at first myself," she laughed. She hadn't meant to sound like Miss Goody Twoshoes.

"You'll have to tell me about it sometime," he said. He went into Miss Dickerson's room. See what you missed, girl, by getting your homeroom changed?

She watched for him in all her classes but didn't see him until history. His presence filled the room. She remembered him now, he was very smart, but she couldn't think of his name.

He sat two rows behind her and one desk over. She dropped her pencil so she could glance at him when she picked it up. He was watching her. His eyes turned on a fire behind her face. Why had she looked? She was still in confusion between Kay's idea that boys like to be noticed and Sammy's declaration that boys are more interested if they think you are not interested.

Well, Sammy was a boy and he ought to know. But, then, Kay always had several boyfriends. Maybe it depended on the boy.

Miss Dickerson began calling names and giving out report cards. Sara was surprised that she had forgotten all about it. Whatever his name was, he had taken her mind off history completely.

"Sara Jane Chambers."

Sara was nervous as she walked up and took her report card. Miss Dickerson had shown no reaction to the note or the outline. Sara couldn't even remember clearly what she had written in the note. The only thing she could fathom was that Miss Dickerson had made no gibes.

Sara held the card as though it were a porcupine. Her face was red again. Obviously, since she had been Miss Dickerson's quarry for the year, everyone was looking at her.

As quickly as possible, she resettled at her desk and opened the card. She put mental fingers in the dikes of her eyes to hold back an expected flood of tears.

"C." Quarter grade "B" and final grade "C." She could scarcely believe it. The card read D-D-D-B-C for the year. She bit her lip to keep from either crying or laughing. She was ready to do both. Miss Dickerson gave out the last card as the bell rang.

Sara quickly remembered the boy. She had meant to get his name when he went up for his report card, but the shock of getting a passing grade had made her forget him. All she knew was that his name started with something after "Chambers." She had a sinking feeling. It was the last day of school and there would be no chance to develop a friendship.

As his pale blue shirt moved toward the door, she stepped quickly to the doorway.

"Hey, listen." She touched the back of his shirt. He turned. When he saw it was Sara, he smiled. His quick response made her stammer.

"Uh. There's this party tonight. A spend-the-night-party at Jean's. You know, Jean Jones? I mean, the girls are spending the night." She stopped and took a deep breath. "Well, some of the guys are coming over around seven for hamburgers. You don't have to come as my, you know, date. But I just thought maybe you would like to come."

Her heart had fallen back into her chest cavity but it

was rat-tat-tatting madly. Darts of pain were actually shooting behind her eyes.

"Sounds like fun," he said. "Thanks for asking me. If I can go, I will see you there."

She barely heard what he was saying. Her expression was frozen on her face and she hoped she didn't look as frightened as she felt. Were boys this jittery when they asked girls out? He walked away and she grasped the arm of a girl nearby.

"What's his name, that boy in the blue shirt?" She nodded her head to where he was weaving his way down the hall.

"Francis. Francis Farnesworth."

Sara grimaced. Yes, that was the name and she'd never liked it. "Don't they call him Frank or something?"

"Not that I know of." The girl turned away and began talking to someone else.

The blue shirt was now lost in the crowd. Sara turned back to speak to Miss Dickerson. Several students were gathered around the teacher's desk, students who had evidently had a better year with Miss Dickerson than Sara. Sara hesitated. She was too fluttery to go plunging in among the others. She would surely start to cry. Thank you, Miss Dickerson, she said quietly to herself.

As soon as she could, Sara found Kay and told her about Francis Farnesworth and her history grade, in that order.

"All year," she scolded herself. "And I didn't even notice him until today!"

"Well, maybe you weren't ready for him until today," Kay said.

"But, what good will it do me now? I won't see him all summer."

"Just please make up your mind not to nurse him in your thoughts all summer," Kay pleaded. "You'll get him all out of proportion and in the fall he won't fit your image. Why don't you ask him to the party?"

Sara stumbled and bumbled almost as much as when she had asked him.

"I did," she blurted.

"You did?" Kay's voice elevated to a squeal. "Why didn't you say so?" Kay took Sara's hands and jumped around.

"Maybe I shouldn't have asked him."

"What? Of course you should. The worst he can do is not come."

"That's what I'm afraid of." She was wavering again. She had shown her interest in him by asking.

"Oh, calm down. Sammy's coming." Kay said it knowing what good friends Sara and Sammy were. Kay didn't know what a tease Sammy could be. Sara's reserve came in a tidal wave. She wouldn't go. How could she? No one knew what energy it took to bulldoze her shyness.

Even though she hadn't noticed Francis Farnesworth she had been trying to notice people. She had put forth conscious effort to respond when spoken to and to not let conversations drop dead when they came her way. But sometimes her carapace seemed thick and strong and comforting.

"I'm going to Jean's now. Why don't you come on over early and help us get ready?"

"Okay," Sara said, not at all sure what she would do.

They parted at the corner, Kay going to Jean's and Sara to her own house. Sara felt confused and unreal. First she had been so conscious of Francis Farnesworth that she had forgotten history. Then she had been so conscious of history that she had forgotten Francis Farnesworth.

What a stupid name, anyway. She gave a stone a whack with her toe. If I knew him I'd have to call him Frank. Cradling the stone between her feet, she hop-hop-hopped up the stairs to the byway. Every time Francis Farnesworth crossed her mind she tried to flick him away. Kay was right. Dwelling on him would make him go out of focus. He would become cuter and sweeter and more desirable and if he didn't come to the party it would get the summer off to a wrong start. And this summer was going to be perfect. On Monday she would start working with Dr. Montini!

She didn't think of the Kellermans until she passed Sammy's house. She tried to squeeze them out of her mind. If she wasn't going to fret about Francis Farnesworth, she wasn't going to fret about the Kellermans either. She just hoped with all her heart that Dave's stealing was a one-time-only trip.

Flipping through the things in her closet, her confidence began rising. She would go to the party. She would definitely go. A smile stretched across her mouth.

Thinking of it, she was filled with anticipation. Whoever was there, she would just pretend that she was self-assured enough to carry on an interesting and intelligent conversation.

She went through a routine with Mr. Imaginary. Coincidentally, he looked like Francis Farnesworth.

"I can't imagine why I haven't noticed you before," she would say.

"Well, I've been here," he would say. Or, perhaps, "Well, I've been noticing you."

"What do you do when you haven't got your nose in a book?" she would ask.

"I play all the sports."

No. Cross that out. If he played all the sports she would know who he was, even if she didn't actually know him. It would give her a broad base for conversation. What if he was interested in something she didn't care a thing about, like cars? Oooh. She had read that the best way to maintain any conversation was to be interested in the other person and keep him talking about himself.

"Oh, I like to tinker around with my car," he would say.

"Well, that's something I don't know much about, but it sounds fascinating." She was satisfied with that response, except for the "well." She would have to learn to talk without saying "well" so many times. Someone would be sure to say, "that's a deep subject for such a shallow mind." That would put her off and she would lose the gist of the conversation.

She called her mother at work to remind her about the party.

"I'll put the name, address, and phone number here by the telephone so you'll know where I am," Sara said. "And by the way, I got a 'C' in history. 'B' for the quarter and 'C' for the year."

"You see, Miss Dickerson isn't such a mean old bag after all, is she?" Sara could feel her mother oozing through the wire, trying to hang on to the newfound compatibility.

Sara patted Mutt as she went out the door. Her shyness almost grabbed her as she started off alone. She wasn't really friends with Jean. She wasn't real friends with anyone but Kay and Sammy. And, once upon a time, Dave Kellerman.

She began kicking a stone. It was the first time she had ever kicked a stone going *away* from home. She kicked away Dave Kellerman and smiled. All kinds of new things were happening. Francis Farnesworth. Dr. Montini. Even her mother; they were beginning to like each other again. And she did have Kay and Sammy and, now, Jean. Her self-assurance returned.

At Jean's, several girls were in the kitchen. The room was strewn with the makings of salad and hamburgers.

"Come on, dive in," Jean said. "Put your stuff in that

room at the top of the stairs and wash your hands and help with the patties."

"How many are coming?" Sara asked when she had her hands on the meat. She had never seen so much ground beef in one pile.

"I have no idea," Jean said.

"You mean your mother let you have a party without even knowing how many are coming?"

"I know how many girls," she said. "But everyone was helping me ask boys and we don't know how many will come."

Sara was relieved. Even though Kay had told her they could invite someone she had felt rather presumptuous in asking Francis Farnesworth—not that he would come.

"Mother lets me have four parties a year," Jean was saying. Four parties a year. It sounded so organized.

A few boys arrived before they were through with the patties and Jean excused herself to be hostess. Sara's hands were suffering frostbite from the cold hamburger meat.

"Look." Kay was up to her elbows mixing tossed salad by hand. Sara followed the direction of Kay's nudge, certain that Kay had already spotted her male interest for the night.

"It's him," Kay said. Sara turned and saw Francis. She plunged her hands back into the ground beef and vigorously beat out another patty.

"Go on out there," Kay said. Sara shook her head. "Come on. I'll help you with him if you'll help me with Sammy."

"Who?"

"Don't look so startled. I've liked Sammy for a long time."

Sara's heart was playing volley ball all through her chest. She conversed with herself, ignoring Kay's pleadings to leave the kitchen. I can't stand a whole party with him here. Yes, you can. You will talk to him and act like a normal, intelligent human being. Normal, ahhhch! No one has ever accused me of that yet.

She finished the patties with a vengeance and her fingers scraped the bowl in frantic surprise when she found the bottom. Kay had finished making the salad and left.

"Wash your hands and join the party," someone said. It was Jean's mother. "That's the last of it." Sara washed her hands like Lady Macbeth, stalling for time.

"Oh, go on, now." Mrs. Jones turned off the water and thrust a towel into Sara's hands. "No one here bites."

If her reluctance was that obvious, Sara decided she'd better go upstairs and calm herself. She was rounding the newel-post when Sammy caught her.

"Hey, Sara Jane, baby. I didn't know you were here." He gallantly put his arm around her waist and scooped her toward the people.

"I'm here, all right," she smiled faintly. There were people grouped all around the living room and out on the porch and in the yard. Her eyes darted around; he wasn't in the living room. She made herself relax. No one here bites. Not even Francis Farnesworth. She recognized most of the kids. None of them looked vicious.

"There you are," Kay swooped her by the elbow in an attempt to steer her. "It's so crowded in here, let's go out on the porch." But Sara outmaneuvered Kay. A quick glance to the porch had revealed a white-with-blue-striped shirt filled with Francis Farnesworth.

"Maybe later," Sara smiled a you-stay-out-of-this smile. In an instant Sara's smile became genuine. Kay could take it either way. If Sara wouldn't go to the porch, Kay could stay with Sara. And Sammy. It amused Sara to know that Kay was playing it Sammy's way, feigning casual disinterest.

Sara stood, exchanging banter with Sammy and Kay

and others who meandered by. Talking with Sammy was a good way to get into the spirit of things without feeling out of her element. When she was quite ready, she disengaged herself and strolled onto the porch. Some of the boys were in the yard pitching horseshoes and other boys and girls stood around watching.

Clang. The sound of a ringer reverberated through the air.

Francis was sitting on the porch swing, gliding gently back and forth. He was in conversation with several people. He didn't see Sara. I ought to go over and say I am glad he could come. The mere thought caused her to tuck her head inside her shell.

Purposefully, she walked down the steps and became engrossed in horseshoes.

17

SARA stationed herself where she could, on pretense of watching horseshoes, keep an eye on the porch. Francis seemed to be enjoying the swing. As she kept her eyes on both the game and Francis Farnesworth she chatted with other horseshoe spectators. She had lost the self-conscious feeling that everyone was looking at her, waiting for her to do something foolish.

Jean called for them to come eat. Everyone crowded around the table. Francis was in line behind her somewhere.

Filling her plate, she balanced it in one hand while she picked up her drink with the other. She juggled her way to the porch and sat down, hopefully, on the swing.

Sammy came and sat beside her. She talked with Sammy

while cursing him in her mind. There was room for only two on the swing.

Francis came up on the porch and perched on the railing near the swing.

"You've been so busy flitting around like a butterfly I've hardly seen you," he spoke directly to Sara.

"Watch that you don't knock your plate over," she said, fluffing over the "not seeing" bit. "It's too good to waste."

Francis was alternately balancing his drink cup and his plate on the narrow railing. His mouth was full of food, but he smiled.

Sara resumed her conversation with Sammy, casually pushing her foot against the porch floor to give the swing motion. Sammy went to refill his plate and Sara caught her breath as Francis moved onto the swing beside her.

"I got enough to last me a while," he said. His plate was indeed overflowing.

"I see you did," Sara laughed.

"I didn't want to have to be interrupted while you told me about Miss Dickerson." Sara closed her eyes briefly, not believing her luck. He really was interested in her. Francis settled back in the corner of the swing, sitting a little cockeyed so he could face her.

"There's really not anything to tell," Sara began. "We had this misunderstanding and she sort of took it out on me. It upset me a lot at first, but then I realized that she had feelings and problems just like anyone else. Then I quit minding so much." She didn't tell him she had only quit minding this very week.

"I don't think I could be so nice about anyone who took so many digs at me," he said. "She was really wicked sometimes, and you never seemed to do anything to deserve it. Everyone was wondering."

"Oh, dear, you mean it's the talk of the school?" She almost didn't say it out loud, but decided it was all right.

"Not the whole school. But the class, at least."

"Thank goodness it's over. And I passed."

"Me, too. Of course, I never have had to worry about passing or not. I manage to do fairly well."

"I figured you did." She threw this out calculatingly. Forget the "how come I've never noticed you" business. Let him think she had noticed.

"How do you figure that?"

"I just think you must be pretty smart." She watched him blush from the compliment. "What do you do when you haven't got your nose in a book?"

"I have a paper route and I fool around with amateur radio."

She made a mental note to find out about the paper route. Perhaps it was close enough for pleasant summer walks with Mutt.

"You're a ham?" That question was about the extent of her knowledge of amateur radio, but he was pleased.

"Yup. I've just gotten my own license."

"Oh?"

"You have to be sixteen to be licensed. Before that my dad was licensed; then anyone in the family could use the equipment under his supervision."

"All that equipment is pretty expensive, isn't it?" That was a question that didn't sound too dumb.

"That's why I have a paper route. I'm hoping to get a car soon. That way I could handle two or three times the number of papers and get a larger route."

There goes my rendezvous, she thought. If he's in a car with a bigger route . . .

"Where do you have your equipment?" she asked. She might as well settle down and learn about ham radio. He was obviously pleased at her interest. She caught herself letting her attention lapse while still looking attentive.

"Pass that by me again," she said. She was determined to be honest. She would listen sincerely and try to understand what he was saying, or else she would admit that she wasn't really interested. She had learned a lot the past few weeks, trying to listen when people talked rather than being self-conscious and trying to think of what she could possibly say in return. Genuine interest was the thing that really worked. All it was, was caring.

"What about you?" he asked finally. "What do you do when you are not taking barbs from Miss Dickerson?"

"I like sports, football, baseball, basketball, swimming—the works. And, I like to walk. I like animals, especially dogs and horses. So, of course I like to walk with dogs. I'm going to be a veterinarian."

"Wow," he said. He was jiggling his empty cup in his hand. "I think I'd like something else to drink." He excused himself and didn't offer to refill her cup though it, also, was empty. It was like turning off a switch. She sat for a minute, still pushing her foot against the floor, swinging.

Is he so self-centered that he loses interest as soon as the subject leaves himself? He did not seem that way, even though he had talked a lot about his radio. Or was it football or the veterinary thing that turned him off?

Well, that was just too bad. I won't sit here, though, and look like a fool, waiting for him to come back. She got up and dumped her plate into the garbage can provided. She kept her cup. She would get her own refill when Francis had had time to be gone from the drink table.

She joined a group and entered into their conversation. In a minute, Francis came back to the porch. He had two cups in his hands and looked a little forlorn when he saw that the swing had been taken over by another couple.

He came back, Sara thought in surprise. Now what do I do? She didn't know whether to act like she had noticed or not. He looked at her, half embarrassed, like a little boy who had been caught in mischief. He wrinkled his brow, hunched his shoulders, and held out the extra cup to her.

"Just what I was wanting," she said. She turned her own cup upside down to demonstrate its emptiness.

"I'm sorry. I've been monopolizing you and keeping you from the party and I hadn't meant to at all." His tone was apologetic rather than sarcastic. He didn't join the group. Why, he's afraid of being made a fool of, too, she thought.

"Not at all," she smiled. It was up to her, now, to make him feel comfortable and at ease. She moved over, making room for him in the group, and beckoned for him to join them.

"I just wasn't sure you were coming back," she said. "I didn't want you to feel monopolized, either." She pushed the words out over her desire to retreat.

"I don't know when I've enjoyed talking to anyone more," he said. "You fascinate me."

I fascinate someone? He couldn't have said anything to please her more. They spent the evening together, sometimes mingling with others and sometimes talking just with each other. Instead of being turned off by her ambition to be a vet, he was intrigued.

"Cotton candy girls send me nowhere," he said. "I like a girl who thinks of herself as a whole solid person, not just plaster in someone else's mold."

"Wow, I need you to talk to my mother," Sara said.

"She ought to be proud of you."

"She's trying to be, I guess."

Several times she excused herself for busy work. She wanted to be very careful that he didn't feel trapped.

When she went around gathering up paper plates, cups, and napkins, he helped. He seemed hanging back just a little, as though feeling his way. At least he wasn't forward-marching like Bill Sluker.

Promptly at ten-thirty the boys were shooed away.

"I can't believe it's time already," Francis said. "When will you be home tomorrow? May I call you around noon?" She hurriedly scrawled her phone number for him and a thousand yearnings followed him down the sidewalk.

Clouds of soft wonder engulfed her, but she endeavored to act as though her feet were squarely set on terra firma. "Gee, you're so calm about it," a girl said to her.

"About what?"

"About making a hit with Francis Farnesworth."

"Oh? Was I a hit? We were just talking." She swallowed and pasted innocence on her face. She knew she was a hit. It was strong tonic, too. Kay had kept herself carefully away during most of the evening. Now she nudged Sara, knowingly, but didn't give Sara away to the others.

There was the whole thing of getting ready for bed—taking turns in the shower and setting each other's hair. Everyone was buzzing with the fun of the party.

"I admire you so much," one girl said to Sara. It was a girl whom Sara should have known from school, but had, in fact, only become friendly with tonight.

"What?" Sara said. She couldn't imagine anyone admiring her.

"I just wish I could talk to people as easily as you do."

"What?" Sara said again, feeling rather stupid at the repetition. She wanted to crawl inside her shell and savor the evening.

"Yes," another girl said. "You seem so relaxed and casual, yet interested. You make it seem so easy."

"Are you kidding me?" Sara looked from one to the

other. She was getting the sinking feeling that they were teasing her.

"We mean it. We've all been talking about it. Haven't we?" The girls murmured agreement.

"You seemed so standoffish, but you aren't at all."

"And you saved my neck in biology," Jean said.

Sara was dumbfounded. Were they talking about her? And yet, hadn't she just had a wonderful evening? She was beginning to believe them just a little. She had tried to learn how to give and apparently she had learned. It was hard to imagine the Sara of a couple of months ago, when she had first seen Gifford Proctor. Or before that, when she met Kay. It was hard to realize that there was a time when she didn't even know how to talk with Kay. If Kay hadn't been a giving person, they would never have become friends.

"I don't talk to people easily at all," she said. "In fact, I'm trying to learn. I just listen and try to be really interested in whatever they are saying."

"Francis Farnesworth!" a girl sighed.

"What's so great about him?" Sara asked. Of course, she thought he was marvelous but she wanted to hear them say so.

Several of the girls joined in with comments about Francis.

"Doesn't anybody call him Frank?" Sara asked. The name still bothered her a little. Francis Farnesworth.

"Some of the guys call him Francisco, but he's just plain Francis."

Sara rolled "Francisco" around on her tongue while she soaked up the information. Had she been blind to him because he wasn't on one of the athletic teams or because he hadn't paid any attention to her until today? She had been so absorbed in herself that she had not been caring, really, about anyone else. She was going to have to broaden her vision. Maybe Kay was right. Maybe she hadn't been ready for him until today. But from now on she was going to be ready for anything. No telling how much else she had missed.

18

Sara and Kay left for home at eleven so that Sara would be home by noon.

"What if he doesn't call?" Kay asked.

"I'm not even going to think about that," Sara answered. But she was really counting on that phone call.

"I still can't get over it, though," she continued. "Everybody thinking that I am so at ease with people."

"You've learned to be."

"But I wasn't at ease at all. Butter was churning inside. Absolutely curdled."

"It didn't show. You seemed easy. Even Sammy said so."

"What did Sammy have to say?" Sara smiled. Just the thought of Sammy made her comfortable. He hadn't teased her at all.

"He said, 'Look at Sara Jane. Maybe now she'll play football again.' " Kay laughed. Sara knew the thought of Sammy gave Kay good feelings, too.

"Did you make your mark?" Sara hadn't asked in front of the other girls.

"I think so. Oh, I hope so." Kay shivered with delight. "I'm going in easy, playing hard to get. He's sympathizing with me because you made such a hit with Francis. He thinks I like Francis." They both laughed at Kay's success in playing Sammy's own game.

Sara began, absently, to kick a stone. But, this time the stone was definitely a friend.

"What are you doing?" Kay intruded on the solitude. Sara had momentarily forgotten that Kay was even there. It had been just Sara, the stone, and Francis.

"Just kicking a rock," Sara said with derision. She hunched her shoulders and tried to mask her embarrassment. They walked along quietly for another moment. Sara was relieved that she had eased out of that situation.

"You weren't just kicking a rock," Kay broke the silence. "There was something special about it and I want to know what it is."

Sara gave the stone a whamming, uncharacteristic kick to prove she was just kicking a rock.

"What could possibly be special about kicking a rock? Kicking a rock is kicking a rock." Sara had been sharing things with Kay lately, everything but stone kicking and the fact that Dave Kellerman was a thief. Sara wasn't afraid of sounding silly or kooky. Kay would be friend enough to understand that. But stone kicking was a link to the old Sara. As they walked along she scolded her toe away from other stones.

Kay, however, began kicking a stone. Awkwardly, Kay inched up and got set each time before kicking. Sara gritted her teeth and tried to keep talking about other things.

"It has really been a good year," she said. "Rather, a good spring. Ever since Gifford Proctor. And the day we had hysterics about our fathers."

Kay's rock skittered into the street and Kay retrieved it by hand and placed it for the next kick. At the end of the block, Kay left the stone and picked up another when she had crossed the street.

"It all boils down to understanding," Sara said, practically talking to herself. Kay wasn't holding up her share of the conversation. Her full concentration was going into stone kicking.

"You have to understand yourself before you can understand other people." Sara was thinking of her mother and her father and Joyce and Lowe and even Miss Parmalee Dickerson. All the people she had misunderstood because she had misunderstood herself.

"Why don't you try to get it across the street?" Sara said when Kay abandoned her stone at the next intersection.

"How would I get it up the curb?"

Sara's expert toe gave the stone a swift kick and it skittered across the street and came to rest almost against the curb.

"Lucky kick," Kay surmised aloud.

At the opposite curb, Sara put one foot alongside the stone and quickly drew the other up, giving it an "Attention" snap. Without breaking rhythm she broad-jumped up the curb with the stone nestled between the arches of her shoes.

"Now, kick it," she told Kay.

"Don't tell me you learned to do that without practice," Kay said. Kay was like a doctor trying to examine your throat. She was going to do it if it choked you. Probe, probe, probe.

Sara smiled. Kay reminded Sara of a Robert Frost poem —"something there is that doesn't like a wall." Kay was pounding down all of Sara's walls. "It's just a game I made up," Sara said, masking her feelings about the ritual in casualness.

Spoken aloud, the rules Sara had devised for her solitary game of stone kicking sounded foolish. But Kay seemed to find it fun. Kay was on her seventh stone by the time she kicked it up to the rock garden.

"Usually, I only keep the stones that I have kicked all the way home," Sara said.

"You mean you can kick the same stone all the way?" Kay was awed.

"Certainly. It took a while, though. But since this is your first stone . . ." Sara stooped to pick up Kay's stone.

"Let me," Kay said. "Please. Let me." Kay cradled the stone in her hands and then set it down in the rock garden. "It's like making a touchdown," she added.

It seemed so ridiculous that Sara almost laughed. It was, after all, just a game. Yet she had followed it as a ritual all year. Sara went around to the front with Kay to walk part way up the long hill. Miss Parmalee Dickerson was just getting out of her car with a bag of groceries.

"Hi, Miss Dickerson," Sara called out with genuine cheerfulness.

"Hello, Sara Jane," Miss Dickerson replied.

Kay looked at Sara and raised her eyebrows. Sara, filled with a strange exhilaration, smiled. Sammy and the gang were playing football in the lot. Someone missed a pass and the ball tumbled out onto the sidewalk. Quickly and easily Sara scooped the ball into her hands.

"Go out for a long one, Sam," she called. The ball felt

comfortable gripped in her fingers, her arm was at ease as she threw a long, accurate pass. "Maybe she'll play football again," Sammy had said to Kay. Well, maybe she would, at that.

Kay was walking up the hill backwards, watching Sara.

"Sara, you're hopeless," Kay called.

Sara smiled and waved one last time. She didn't feel hopeless. Somehow, something great had been accomplished this spring.